©Nao Watanuki

Toshio Satou

Illustration by
Nao Watanuki

D1510874

Suppose
a **Kid** from the **Last Dungeon**
Boonies Moved to a **Starter Town**

Abandon all common sense, ye who enter here! Welcome to Lloyd's hometown!

©Nao Watanuki

Is this the legendary village of Kunlun...?!

"Let's put the world back the way it was and finally have real peace."

Lena Eug
Self-proclaimed Dwarf King. Old acquaintance of Alka's. Knows a lot about the world's mysteries.

©Nao Watanuki

"Can't it wait awhile longer?"

©Nao Watanuki

[CONTENTS]

PROLOGUE 001

CHAPTER 1 An Unfathomable Homecoming: Suppose Someone
Suggested Making a Day Trip to Neverland 009

CHAPTER 2 A Big Blow: Suppose a Once-Respected Classmate
Had Become Unrecognizable at a School Reunion 047

CHAPTER 3 A Major Obstacle: Suppose You Needed to Win a
Game of Chess with No Rooks or Bishops 107

CHAPTER 4 To the Rescue: Suppose a Hero Always Showed Up
Late...Even if He Was Unaware of It Himself 173

Suppose a Kid from the Last Dungeon Boonies Moved to a Starter Town

5

Toshio Satou

Illustration by
Nao Watanuki

YEN ON
NEW YORK

Suppose a Kid from the LAST DUNGEON ⑤ BOONIES Moved to a Starter Town

TOSHIO SATOU

Translation by Andrew Cunningham
Cover art by Nao Watanuki

TATOEBA LAST DUNGEON MAENO MURANO SHOUNEN GA JYOBAN NO MACHI DE
KURASUYOUNA MONOGATARI volume 5
Copyright © 2018 Toshio Satou
Illustrations copyright © 2018 Nao Watanuki
All rights reserved.
Original Japanese edition published in 2018 by SB Creative Corp.

This English edition is published by arrangement with SB Creative Corp., Tokyo in care of Tuttle-Mori Agency, Inc., Tokyo.

English translation © 2021 by Yen Press, LLC

Yen On
150 West 30th Street, 19th Floor
New York, NY 10001

Visit us at yenpress.com · facebook.com/yenpress · twitter.com/yenpress
yenpress.tumblr.com · instagram.com/yenpress

First Yen On Edition: March 2021

Yen On is an imprint of Yen Press, LLC.
The Yen On name and logo are trademarks of Yen Press, LLC.

The publisher is not responsible for websites (or their content) that are not owned by the publisher.

Library of Congress Cataloging-in-Publication Data
Names: Satou, Toshio, author. | Watanuki, Nao, illustrator. | Cunningham, Andrew, 1979– translator.
Title: Suppose a kid from the last dungeon boonies moved to a starter town / Toshio Satou ; illustration by Nao Watanuki ; translation by Andrew Cunningham.
Other titles: Tatoeba last dungeon maeno murano shounen ga jyoban no machi de kurasuyouna. English
Description: First Yen On edition. | New York, NY : Yen ON, 2019–
Identifiers: LCCN 2019030186 | ISBN 9781975305666 (v. 1 ; trade paperback) |
ISBN 9781975306236 (v. 2 ; trade paperback) | ISBN 9781975313043 (v. 3 ; trade paperback) |
ISBN 9781975313296 (v. 4 ; trade paperback) | ISBN 9781975313319 (v. 5 ; trade paperback)
Subjects: CYAC: Adventure and adventurers—Fiction. | Self-esteem—Fiction.
Classification: LCC PZ7.1.S266 Tat 2019 | DDC [Fic]—dc23

LC record available at https://lccn.loc.gov/2019030186

ISBNs: 978-1-9753-1331-9 (paperback)
978-1-9753-1332-6 (ebook)

10 9 8 7 6 5 4 3 2 1

LSC-C

Printed in the United States of America

Character Profiles

Alka

Chief of the town of legend. Dotes on Lloyd like he's her own son. Seems to have history with the enigma named Sou.

Lloyd Belladonna

Excessively strong villager raised in the town of legend. His accidental accomplishments in the military drew the ire of some upperclassmen.

Marie the Witch

Disguises herself as an information broker on the East Side but is actually the princess of the Azami Kingdom. Enjoys living with Lloyd too much to drop the pretense.

©Nao Watanuki

Allan Lidocaine

Son of a decorated noble family. Meeting Lloyd has only spread his fame.

Riho Flavin

Skilled mercenary. In it for the money. Lately seems preoccupied with Lloyd's every move.

Selen Hemein

Former Cursed Belt Princess. Devoted to Lloyd, who changed her destiny. ♥

Merthophan Dextro

Former Azami soldier. Currently living in Kunlun as penance for his crimes.

Choline Sterase

A female instructor at the military academy. Flummoxed by the powerful new students.

Phyllo Quinone

A martial artist who admires Lloyd. Was trained by someone from Kunlun.

Lena Eug

Self-proclaimed Dwarf King. Old acquaintance of Alka's. Has the world's secrets in her grasp.

Shouma

A Kunlun villager. Prone to yammering about "passion." Currently traveling the world.

Sou

An enigmatic mystery man. No two people come away with the same impression of him.

The reception room at the Azami castle was a solemn space used to greet visiting dignitaries.

The king of Azami was sitting behind a desk so intricately carved, it gave movers nightmares.

He was projecting a noble, dignified air, but there was a piercing glare in his eyes.

The grim figure guarding the king was genuinely imposing.

He had a square face and a rock-solid build. The former head of the royal guards, he was currently an instructor at the military academy. Colonel Chrome Molybdenum.

Joining them were Azami's foremost expert on healing magic, Colonel Choline Sterase, and the master of water magic, Mena Quinone. Three of the Azami military's top minds in one room.

All eyes were on a tanned young man with a hat pulled low over his eyes.

He was *not* dressed for the occasion—instead, he wore a loose shirt, sturdy pants, and thick-soled shoes, as if he were on a hike.

Undaunted in the face of their knifelike stares, he grinned, as if delighted by the entire situation.

"It's a real honor to meet you, Your Majesty! I—"

"Remove your hat and state your name," Chrome barked.

"Whoops, my bad!" Like he'd been waiting for someone to call him on it, the man whipped off his hat and bobbed his head. "They call me Shouma. I'm here on behalf of the Jiou Empire!"

This flippant manner provoked a rage Chrome did not even try to disguise. He huffed loudly. "Sorry, but do you *really* work for them?"

Shouma yanked a thick sheet of paper out of his pocket—once again, as if he'd been waiting for this moment. "Official papers from Jiou! Signed by the emperor himself, with my name right here! See?"

He held it out with a ninety-degree bow as if he were proffering a love letter. Chrome took it, checked it to see if it was safe, then handed it to the king.

The king grunted once, then passed it directly back to Shouma.

"That is certainly the seal of the Jiou emperor. Apologies for doubting your word."

"Not at all! I am dressed like this, after all! I come waltzing in with my hat still on, and anyone would get suspicious!"

Then why didn't he change? Before anyone could ask the obvious question, Shouma rattled on.

"Sadly, the Jiou Empire and Azami Kingdom haven't been on the best of terms lately, so if I rolled in with loads of pomp and circumstance, I figured I'd just piss everyone off and set a million schemes churning, so I decided to dress down! A tough choice, I assure you."

This seemed highly unlikely.

However, the king gave Shouma a look of great sympathy.

"Oh! How thoughtful of you. The consideration is appreciated."

"What a generous ruler you are! They don't call you the world's most accessible king for nothing! Such passion!"

Before Shouma could butter the king up any more, Colonel Choline stepped in.

"I hate to nag, but ya might wanna get to the point."

Unperturbed by her evident skepticism, Shouma made a show of surprise—again, like he'd been waiting for this cue.

"Oh! So sorry! Gotta be professional here. I think I put it between the dry rice and the jerky... There it is!"

Shouma produced something out of his bag.

Between the wax paper packaging and the imposing seal, it was clear this was important.

"Why is something that crucial stowed with your provisions?!"

"Best place to hide something obviously valuable!"

Shouma held out the parcel. It smelled faintly of seasonings.

The king accepted it and perused the contents.

Growing impatient, Chrome asked, "Your Majesty, what does it say?"

"Hmm, it suggests holding an exhibition match in Azami with an eye to improving international relations."

"I'm sure you're all perfectly aware of this," Shouma said, "but the cross-continental railway between Jiou and Azami is almost complete."

Construction had been halted as tensions rose but had resumed recently, and it was now being treated as a symbol of their improved relationship.

"It's already done! They got the ceremony planned and the tape ordered so someone can pop by and cut it."

"And on that occasion, the emperor of Jiou would like to take the railroad to Azami, as a demonstration of our newfound friendship."

Shouma bowed low.

"That, I get," Chrome said. "But why an exhibition match?"

Shouma had anticipated that question, too.

"I'm afraid there are still many Jiou citizens who harbor resentment toward Azami," he explained. "I imagine it's the same on your side."

"Certainly...and regrettably."

"And when your people work up a head of steam, well—to put it bluntly—a proxy war can help 'em blow off that steam. Naturally, nothing is riding on the match's outcome, and it's purely for entertainment purposes." Shouma bowed again.

"Hmm, well, if neither of us harbors a grudge about the outcome, it should be acceptable."

©Nao Watanuki

"So you agree to the match?"

"Yes, tell the emperor I'm on board. Choline, would you mind preparing an arena and making the necessary arrangements?"

Choline snapped to attention. "I'm the best at that! Leave it to me."

The king nodded, pleased, and turned back to Shouma.

"Thank the Jiou emperor for his generous suggestion, and tell him we'll make a grand show of things. A perfect chance to demonstrate the power of our friendship! Let him know the answer, and inform him we'll be in touch with the detailed rules later."

The king wrote out a proper reply and handed it to Shouma.

"Such passion! Honestly, I didn't expect you to agree to it so readily."

"It is a king's duty to alleviate the anxiety of his citizens. I consider this match our top priority!"

The king bowed, and Shouma returned the favor.

"Great! I'll let him know your passionate response!"

Without ever dropping his cheery manner, Shouma left the reception room.

Soldiers hastily saw him out—while keeping a watchful eye on him.

With the boisterous emissary gone, there was a moment of peace. Chrome let out a post-work sigh.

"That went easily enough."

"Yes, we all braced ourselves when an emissary from Jiou arrived, but thankfully it ended without issue."

The king kept the dignified look on his face but leaned back in his chair, exhaling in relief.

"Yeah," Mena said, nodding in agreement. "There was always the possibility he'd just go for your throat!"

"Geez, don't scare me like that, Mena," Choline joked. "Well, all's well that ends well."

Mena finger-gunned her. "Anything happens, my water magic can spit fire!"

"That'd be the day!" Choline laughed.

"Come now," Chrome said in his best dad voice. "No goofing off in front of the king."

"Right, sorry," Mena apologized, totally blowing him off. "Still, that kid never once dropped his smile. Takes a lot of balls to face down these grim soldiers and my cute factor without batting an eye!"

Choline frowned, shaking her head at Mena's bad manners.

"Mena, honey, you aren't the only cute one here."

"Yikes, my bad, *our* cute factor."

They high-fived. Clearly, it hadn't been Mena's manners Choline had objected to.

Chrome let out the same sigh of every dad who can't get his daughters to listen...and the king gave him a sympathetic pat on the shoulder. The king himself was busy being studiously ignored by his own daughter at present. See the previous volume to learn why!

Hearing his exhale, Choline turned back to Chrome.

"Oh, yeah, Chrome, that kid was pretty strong, right?"

Chrome had seen enough combat that he could size up an opponent's abilities at a glance. And he did not look happy here.

"I didn't get anything off him...," he admitted, scratching his neck.

"Nothin'? Not strong *or* weak?"

"How's that work?" Mena asked, narrowing her smiley eyes. "Are your sensors on the fritz? Have you been so busy lately you forgot to do some routine maintenance?"

"They're organic, so no...," Chrome said sullenly. "If you girls would take things seriously, maybe I wouldn't be so strung out all the time."

Both grown women stuck their tongues out at him.

Chrome let out another sigh and called out to the soldiers around them.

"Just like his manner, he's a hard man to get a read on. He may be hiding his true strength. Maintain the utmost caution around him."

The soldiers all barked their understanding.

The king seemed to be mulling things over.

"Your Majesty?"

"This exhibition match... We should put our finest warrior in it. And that means the dragon slayer himself, Allan Toin Lidocaine."

Chrome winced.

Allan Toin Lidocaine was a military cadet from an aristocratic background. Strong arms and an ugly mug that made him look far older than he actually was.

Rumor had it he'd knocked down dozens of dragons with his voice alone during a recent dungeon incident, and the king had personally granted him the dragon slayer title.

In actual fact, the dragons had just collapsed with uncanny timing as a result of a completely different battle...and Chrome felt sorry for the poor boy, laden with an epithet that was far too grand for him.

"Poor Allan...," Choline said.

"Well, it's just an exhibition. Nothing riding on it, so it doesn't matter who we put in it," Mena added.

"Let's get planning!" the king announced and stormed out of the room.

"There he goes... Let's hope his dedication doesn't blow things out of proportion again. Mm? What's wrong, Choline?"

As Chrome made to follow the king, he noticed an unusually serious look on Choline's face.

"I was just thinking about...the Jiou Empire. What would Merthophan think if he heard this?"

Merthophan Dextro—once a colonel in the Azami military, he'd worked alongside Choline.

He'd been a fierce patriot, but a demon lord had taken advantage of that patriotism, and he'd been tricked into placing the country he loved in dire peril.

Now he was paying for his crimes in a distant land.

"Well, no sense cryin' about it now! We got a match to plan and a railroad to open! Mountains of work!"

Instantly snapping back to her usual self, Choline raced out of the room.

"I wonder what he's doing now," Chrome muttered. His thoughts on his former colleague, he glanced out the window, staring into the distant sky.

A few days after the proposal for this exhibition...

At Marie the Witch's shop on the East Side, a CLOSED sign dangled on the doorknob in the middle of the day.

"All packed! A bit of a tight fit, but I definitely need all of this, so..."

Marie, the shop's owner, wore a black robe and hat that just screamed *witch*. There was an intricate, expensive-looking brooch pinned to her outfit. She was currently struggling with a huge suitcase—getting ready for a journey.

She managed to get the clasps on it closed somehow and moved the thing gingerly to the side of the room like she was afraid it would explode. As she did, someone else came in.

"'Sup! You all ready, Marie?"

A slim woman with beady eyes, dressed in light layers that were little better than underwear, flashed a menacing mechanical arm.

"Oh, Riho! You're early."

Her name was Riho Flavin. Hailing from the Flavin district, she put her trademark mithril arm to work earning money as a mercenary. Now she was a military cadet in Azami but always on the lookout for a quick buck—so basically, nothing had changed.

She plopped herself down on a chair like she owned the place, smirking.

"Yeah, I wake up early on days off—earlier than school days, anyway. Heh-heh-heh."

The habit was not unlike a child jumping out of bed on a Saturday to watch their favorite cartoons.

Marie was distinctly uncomfortable.

Why is she so into this?

Riho was generally the type to roll in at the last moment, looking like she didn't wanna be there. Oblivious to Marie's concerns, Riho was rummaging through a small knapsack.

"Uh, Riho, is that all you're bringing?"

It didn't even seem full—quite a disparity between her own over-stuffed suitcase.

"All I need. I can go a couple of days without a change of clothes or underwear, no problem."

"H-how very mercenary...," Marie offered. Not very ladylike, though.

"This is way more important than clothes," Riho said, producing a harvesting knife out of the knapsack. She ran her finger along the blade, checking it for rust.

Even less ladylike.

"Er." Marie gulped. "What's so important about a knife?"

Riho cackled. "Well, we're goin' to the legendary Kunlun, right? Even a random leaf from the woods out back might be a valuable item! And...we might find stuff dropped by the high-level monsters that the villagers hunt! Even a single scale would rake in the dough! Mwa-ha!"

Oh, I get it... In Kunlun, even their staple fish is a dangerous monster called the killer piranha, as is their kindling—they use treant wood. That could be a treasure trove.

They were headed to a place called Kunlun—a secret village in a hidden realm, like something out of a fairy tale.

Recent events had left Kunlun's guardian beast reduced to a shadow of its former self, and their goal was to restore it—but Riho had clearly forgotten all about that.

Marie took off her glasses, rubbing her eyes.

©Nao Watanuki

"Just…don't overdo it," she warned.

The kid grandma hailed from Kunlun, and if everyone was like her, there was no way Riho's schemes would go as planned—but Marie couldn't think of anything that would shake Riho from the scent of gold. She settled for a half-hearted warning.

While Marie was staring in horror at Riho's lack of luggage, a blond beauty came in—Selen.

She went straight to her knees, her fingertips placed together in a triangle before her, her head bowed low.

"In sickness or in health, I swear— I mean, good morning!"

Marie was already at a loss for words.

Had she spent all night rehearsing marriage vows? Marie's cheek twitched.

She's totally convinced herself she's going to meet future in-laws…

Selen paid Marie's consternation no heed. Still on her knees, she started drooling, lost in a fantasy. Her brain had likely moved right past the vows, through the ceremony and the honeymoon, and they were now enjoying the slow life in the country with a gaggle of kids.

Riho was usually the one in charge of vicious put-downs where Selen's delusions were concerned, but…

"I might even sell enough materials from Kunlun to buy a house! Heh…heh…heh…"

…The mercenary was lost in her *own* delusions.

They were counting different chickens, but neither set of 'em were likely to hatch, and both of Marie's cheeks were twitching now. Her heart rate had doubled, too.

"I have one set of marriage paperwork in my jacket, one in my skirt, five in my luggage, all filled out and ready! Just waiting for the official seal of approval! I'm perfectly prepped for this trip! Flawless!"

Sounded like she hadn't brought a change of clothes, either… Unless you could use marriage paperwork in lieu of underwear? Call it a bit avant-garde.

Marie felt like she really should say *something*. She put her hand on her hip, sighing.

"You do remember *why* we're going to Kunlun, right?"

"To meet Lloyd's chosen family!"

"Don't be ridiculous, Selen. We're on a harvesting tour."

"Is there nobody sane left?!" Marie wailed.

A figure loomed over her shoulder, arms dangling limp.

"......Mm."

"Ack! Ph-Phyllo?!"

How long had she been there? This towering, stealthy interloper was the martial artist Phyllo. As quiet as she was expressionless, she had joined the group unnoticed.

"Geez, if you're here, say something! My heart can't take that!"

Marie's heart had been racing to begin with. If humans had a finite number of heartbeats in their lives, the last few minutes had shortened her life expectancy by several years.

Her heart was racing so fast that the vibrations were making her whole chest heave. Chipping away at her life to deliver some fanservice—you gotta respect her commitment.

Not to be outdone, Phyllo puffed out her own chest.

"...The goal of this trip? ...You've all got it wrong."

"Er, oh? Phyllo! You're the last person I expected this from."

"......We're going to battle powerful warriors in the village of legend."

Phyllo snapped into a karate stance. Ready for combat.

Surrounded by people in a world of their own, Marie was forced to give up in defeat.

"Do none of you remember?" This response came from Selen—or at least from something at Selen's waist. "Ladies, our purpose here is my restoration!"

The cursed belt—Vritra. The end of the belt reared up, then dipped downward, as if bobbing its head.

Vritra was the guardian beast of Kunlun, a giant snake that had lost his body. To save himself, he'd been forced to possess the belt around Selen's waist—its leather made from his own skin.

If they left him like this, terrible things might befall Kunlun and the world at large, so the goal of the day was to head to the legendary village and restore him to his original form.

Vritra seemed weirdly on edge—like a caged cat that knows it's about to get vaccinated.

"Are you okay, Vritra?" Selen asked. "You've been awfully quiet lately."

"Nothing to worry about, mistress. I am merely overcome with remorse, having long neglected my duties as Kunlun's guardian beast."

"Oh, that's right! That's why I was trying to cheer you up! Shall I tell you the story of how Lloyd and I first met again?"

"Please, don't! No more! Mistress, I beg you! I can't handle another night of endless stories about Lloyd, lists of his hundred best features..."

Selen had evidently turned Vritra into a captive audience for her Lloyd monologues. It was like having a radio program you found completely uninteresting blasted in stereo twenty-four/seven.

"Selen, you should never be allowed to get a pet."

It might sound cute for a girl to tell a pet all about her crush, but if that went on all night, every night— Well, an overattentive pet owner could wear their pet out by overcaressing it. Poor thing.

Selen stroked her belt like she would a cat, and Vritra flinched, clearly terrified. The fact that Selen meant no harm just made it all the more awkward.

Behind Vritra, the closet started rattling.

"Looks like the kid grandma's here—Kunlun's chief."

Marie scowled at the closet. The chief of Kunlun, Alka, frequently teleported to Azami and back using a crystal in Marie's closet as a gate.

"She's gonna stomp all over my clothes in there again. That idiot!" Maire muttered as if all hope was lost in the world. But today, things seemed a little different.

There was a flash of light, and then the closet door began rattling even harder, shaking violently. Finally, the hinges smashed open, and a tiny little girl with black twin tails came bursting out.

She bounced all over Marie's shop like a superball struck by the hammer of a gold medalist. Marie was hit square in the face; then Selen's belt knocked Alka toward Riho, who dodged smoothly. Finally, Phyllo did a volleyball receive that left Alka's head firmly lodged in the ceiling.

The martial artist looked up at her, hands still clasped together.

"………………Madness," she whispered.

Alka's entrances were always extreme, but this was definitely on a whole new level.

There was a long silence; then Alka started swearing and pried her head out of the ceiling.

"I really didn't think I'd have *this* much trouble controlling my power… Morning, folks."

She sounded like a ghastly monster delivering a surprisingly cordial greeting.

"Oh, that won't let you off the hook!" Selen yelled. "You were like a living cannonball! If Vritra hadn't stepped in, I'd have been sent to a hospital!"

"*Protection* is my middle name, mistress. In return, I merely ask that you stop trying to cheer me up all night long."

Vritra cowed again, and Alka glared at him.

"You always did get spooked by chatty girls," she observed.

"Alka! You've forgotten what you've done to me, but remember the little details? Most vexing."

Vritra did his best to maintain his gentlemanly tone in the face of provocation.

Now that things have settled down a little, it's time for her introduction. Her name is Alka. She might look and sound like an adorable little girl, but she was well over a hundred years old. She served as the chief of Kunlun, but it was highly doubtful she ever did anything chief-like. She teleported over to Azami to see Lloyd basically every day...and who could trust a politician who spent all their time goofing off?

Marie was Alka's student. She was currently clutching her very red nose—injured in the commotion of the kid grandma's entrance. "What's wrong with you now, Master? You usually just settle for trampling on all my clothes, but today you decide to stomp on my entire domicile?!"

"Whoopsie-daisy. If you want me to step all over your clothes so bad, I could go back?"

"No! That's not what I meant just... Hey, I like that one!"

Alka was trampling clothing like a pro wrestler, Marie already on the verge of tears—pretty much the usual deal, so everyone else just watched.

Once she'd stomped everything in the closet, Alka appeared thoroughly satisfied—and explained the reason for her rocket entrance.

"With Vritra not in his true form, my powers have grown unstable! I thought it was still safe, but clearly, we have no time to waste."

"Unstable?"

Alka sat down on a chair and started scarfing down cookies. Maybe bouncing around like a rubber ball made her hungry. Maybe she just wanted cookies.

"I might have to fly here next time...but that would take, like, a full day..."

Riho blinked at this.

"Wait, does that mean we're gonna have to fly to Kunlun? Is it really gonna take all day? I thought we were staying the night! I was planning on hauling back so much loot, I could barely hold it! I don't want to do a lightning round! We'll have time to harvest, right? I don't care how bouncy it makes you, if it cuts into my foraging time..."

"Riho, your motives sound suspect! And you're much too old to be whining like that."

A sound argument from Alka. A rarity. Riho was normally the one talking sense into everyone, but potential earnings had blinded her. Marie shook her head at this role reversal.

Just as the commotion finally died down, the door was flung open, and the main character, Lloyd, came in—out of breath.

"I'm back! I handed out enough medicine to take care of all your regulars while we're away!"

A boy with a gentle smile, Lloyd wiped the sweat from his brow, looked around at everyone, and bowed his head.

"Th-thanks for coming! You're all here early!"

The moment Lloyd's head lowered, Alka—who doted on him— hurled herself forward like an American football player. Less a hug, more a tackle.

"I missed you, Lloyd! I'm so tired after all that bouncing! Can you give my tired legs and chest a massage? Oh, you must be worn out from running around! I'll give you a good full-body grope—urp!"

Belt-form Vritra had snagged Alka by the throat.

"…Grow up, kid grandma. Do you wish to be indicted for sexual harassment? And I fail to see how your chest grew tired—you've got nothing there."

"Tch, with Vritra possessing that belt, it's grown way stronger… How dare you? That last comment is definitely 'in-dite-able'!"

"You can't even say the word! Nothing that emerges from that child-like frame could possibly faze me. You accumulate years but have not grown at all."

Alka snarled, but the belt around her neck wasn't going anywhere. Everyone but Lloyd gave Vritra a round of applause.

At length, Alka was released. "I could have gone for another few hours," Marie muttered.

"Bahhhaahh…," Alka gasped. Once she'd caught her breath, she added, "I was just…kidding. Vritra…are you prepared?"

"In this form, there's nothing I can do to prepare," Vritra said, writhing pointedly. "I have steeled my will. That is all."

Fired up, Riho shouldered her bag. "Let's go! Time's a-wastin'!"

The scent of profit sure made her sound manly.

The next voice they heard was the exact opposite—despite coming from a man.

"Heeeeeeeelp!"

A man well over six feet tall came bursting in the front door. His uncouth face was dripping with sweat, tears, and snot. This was a lot, even for Allan.

"Oh, Allan."

"L-Lloyd! I need your help!"

Allan must have really wanted to get out of this one. He was on the ground, clinging to Lloyd's feet. It was horrifying, like he'd just crawled out of someone's TV set when they tried to watch a cursed video.

"Uh, Allan? We're about to leave. We don't have time for this."

"Get your filthy face away from Lloyd."

".........Mm."

Each of the girls kicked him in turn. Some might enjoy that.

"Ow! Seriously, that hurts! Especially you, Phyllo!"

Marie gave him the sort of look you reserve for a dying puppy.

"What's the matter, Allan?"

He looked up at her, snot dangling, desperate.

"Y-you see, because of that dungeon thing, everyone started calling me the dragon slayer! And now things are getting even worse!"

"Tch. Boo-hoo. Cry me a river. Sucks to be famous, huh? Quit rubbing it in our faces!" Riho snarled (in between kicks).

Allan's brow furrowed further.

"That's not it!" he wailed. "There's nothing fun about this! Every guild in town is bringing me dangerous quests, I get invited to every major event, important people ask me to dine with them, I never get a second to myself! I'm so stressed that I can't even taste the roast beef! Do you know how that feels?"

".......You got a nice meal? Good for you."

Phyllo liked good meals. She started to kick Allan harder. Right in his ribs.

"Gah! Ow, ow, ow! Cut that out! That's not what this is! I'm getting challenged to duels from everyone looking to make a name for themselves! I won the first few, but they're getting worse and worse! Now I got people gunning for my life! Someone actually said I was 'Worth killin' for the rep alone!' What did I do to deserve death?! Am I gonna die without ever getting a girlfriend?!"

Allan's cries did not fall on deaf ears. The heavens might not have listened, but the man chasing him did.

Chrome's square frame loomed in the doorway, a group of burly soldiers in tow.

"I knew you'd be here, Dragon Slayer Allan! Come! Time to work! You've got to meet weapon merchant VIPs for lunch! Dragon Slayer Allan!"

"N—noooo! I don't want any more tasteless meals from the stress! I'm sick of water being the only enjoyable part! Aughhhh!"

His begging was interrupted by ropes—made of magical water—that dragged him into the air.

"Got him! Mwa-ha-ha-ha!"

".........Mena."

It was Phyllo's older sister, Mena, the water magic specialist. She grinned at everyone.

Behind her was Choline, barking orders to the soldiers as they grabbed Allan by the scruff of his neck.

"Come on. Careful with him. He's got that exhibition match coming up. Hands off his face. Stick to body blows if ya gotta get rough."

"Leave my body alone, too! L-Lloyd!"

Allan turned to Lloyd, desperate. The boy nodded.

"I know how you feel, Allan," Lloyd consoled. "Everything leading up to a match can feel stressful. But don't worry! I'll be there to cheer you on."

"That's not my point! I need help!"

But nobody understood his pleas.

A soldier on each limb, Allan was hauled away like movers handling a refrigerator.

"Well, with a face like his, a few scars won't hurt him any!" Mena snarked.

"What about the wounds to my heaaaaart?!" Allan wailed.

The door slammed behind him.

Chrome bowed low. "Sorry you had to witness that," he said. "Pardon the intrusion, Maria...Marie."

Then he looked around the room, rubbing his chin.

"What brings you all here?" Choline asked.

"Yeah, what's going on?" Mena chimed in. "Phyllo's all fired up! Are you going to grab a bite to eat? In that case, count me in!"

"We're going to Kunlun!" Lloyd said.

"""......*Seriously?!*"""

All three of them froze to the spot. Can't blame 'em. Everyone knew Kunlun as the village where the heroes of legend dwelled. This was like saying they were off to Neverland!

And if Kunlun was Neverland, then Lloyd was both Peter Pan and Tinkerbell.

"We're going to restore Vritra to his true form," Lloyd explained. "We'll probably have to ask the dwarfs for help."

"Huh...," Mena said, her eyes—for once—all the way open. She was so stunned that she forgot to make a flippant remark. People who play dumb can *never* handle people who actually are.

Lloyd himself didn't mean to be stupid... He was just stating the honest truth. Quite earnestly.

"R-right," Chrome mumbled, trying to make his brain process this. "Have fun!" he said, failing. He turned to go.

Choline's eyes narrowed. She looked at Alka, then back at Lloyd.

"Kunlun? If I tagged along, could I see him?"

"Him? Ohhh…Merthophan?"

Merthophan.

That name sure got Riho's attention.

"Huh? Seriously? That dude's in Kunlun?"

"Mm, paying for his sins," Alka said solemnly.

"Sorry, Alka—or should I call you Chief? Mind if butt in on this?"

Alka nodded gravely. "I see no reason to object," she said. "Not like there's a capacity limit."

Choline pumped a fist. Chrome shook his head.

"Geez, you're just gonna let the king prep this exhibition match all on his own?"

Choline winced at that idea.

Then Mena stepped up—sounding completely different from her usual self. Mena spent most of her time playing a goofball, tricking people into underestimating her, but when things turned serious or were beyond her comprehension, her true self emerged. This was definitely one of those moments.

"I'll handle the exhibition match. Chrome, you join her if you want."

Choline threw her arms around Mena. After all, Mena *had* been pretty cool.

"Thanks so much! I owe ya one."

"I'll do what I can. Frankly, if I went to a village filled with Lloyds, my mind would be so blown, I'd probably stop breathing." Mena winced. A whole village of people who don't know they're absurd would definitely prove fatal.

Phyllo tugged at her sleeve, worried.

"……Mena."

"Don't worry, Phyllo, you can go. I got work to do."

"…Your personality."

"—whoops!" Like she'd hit a switch, Mena was back to her old imp-ish grin. "Bring back souvenirs! I demand a full review of anything you eat! Chrome, Choline, you'd better pay me back for this! Next payday's gonna be a treat!"

She moonwalked out of Marie's shop.

"Seems like a hard act to maintain…"

"Thanks again, Mena!"

Seeing everything settled, Alka raised her hands high.

"Right, then let's make way for Kunlun!"

"Uh, Master, nobody's gonna survive the teleportation if it goes like your arrival. *Are* we all gonna fly there? Honestly, I really didn't enjoy it last time when you dangled me above the clouds…"

Everyone except Lloyd winced at that last phrase.

Alka just gave her a cheery thumbs-up.

"Don't worry! I prepared a safe means of transport. C'mon!"

She traipsed out of the shop like she was leading a field trip. Looking nervous, everyone followed after her.

"What do you think it is, M'lady Selen?" Riho asked. "I'm kinda spooked…"

"She 'prepared' something? Are we gonna be riding some legendary bird or…Vritra, do you have any idea?"

"I fear not, mistress! Not the slightest hint of a clue! Pray forgive me."

Vritra cowed, fearing Selen's wrath.

"She should never be allowed to have a pet," Riho muttered.

Alka led the way through the North Gate of Azami—the gateway to the continent—and into the woods beyond. This was totally just a hiking trip now, and Riho was getting increasingly skeptical.

"Is there something *in* this forest?" she asked.

"Mm! There's a dwarf waiting for us up ahead. We gotta meet up with her."

"A dwarf? Here?"

Everyone but Lloyd looked aghast.

Dwarves physically resembled humans but were quite short, like human children. They were strong of body and good with their hands, known for making weapons and works of art, and had gifted the world with any number of advanced ironwork techniques...according to legends.

These days, academics speculated that they'd been a tribe of unusually short nomads or had a unique culture that led to them living in caves... Basically, they were treated the same way modern researchers handled legends of Bigfoot. You know how people just say those are either giant apes or a man in a suit? Same thing.

If this kid grandma hadn't been the chief of an equally mythological village, nobody would have believed her.

"A dwarf!" Lloyd exclaimed. "Wow, it's been ages! For some reason, I haven't seen any of them in Azami!"

You wouldn't! Everyone not from Kunlun thought the same thing.

"Oh, right, when you greet a dwarf, make sure you put your eyes on their level. Otherwise, they'll throw axes at you."

Lloyd had mentioned this tip before, but they'd all assumed they'd never need it.

"Nah, Lloyd," Alka corrected. "The one we're about to meet is a little different, so there's no need for that."

"Oh, really? That *is* different!"

"She makes up for it by being kinda whack-a-doodle. If she says anything weird, just pay it *no* attention."

Alka had said this. *The* Alka. The one who tried to summon a world-destroying dragon whenever she got peeved, who turned people into butterflies and frogs without the slightest trace of guilt. If Alka called her a whack-a-doodle...that was like the heavyweight champion of the world going up before a crowd of reporters and going, "Hell no, I don't ever wanna fight that dude again."

It bore remembering, at the least.

Then the belt at Selen's hips—Vritra—spoke up. "You can't mean... Not her! That's the last person alive I want to meet."

He was shaking like a leaf.

"You okay there, Vritra?"

"I am simply dandy, mistress! Just curb the all-night story sessions designed to cheer me up."

Vritra was now shaking even harder. Everyone cringed in sympathy.

A while later, the party emerged into a forest clearing, where they found a small cave.

Alka stopped there.

"Huh?" Marie asked. "Is this our destination? There's nobody here."

Certainly nobody outside the cave. Just the wind making the grass and trees sway.

But...

"...........There is."

"We just can't see them."

Phyllo and Lloyd spoke at the same time. Both of them were excellent at sensing when people were nearby, so everyone grew tense.

Alka shook her head, sighing.

"We know you're here!" she called, addressing empty air. "Quit horsin' around."

There was a sudden *voom*...and then a girl was standing there. Everyone let out a silent screech.

"You revealed my trick way too fast!" the young woman exclaimed, scowling at Alka.

She was wearing a sturdy helmet and unadorned glass goggles. There was a lively gleam to her eyes and an indomitable grin on her face that flashed her canines—and the stick of a lollipop dangling out of one side of her mouth.

She was wearing some sort of uniform, a bit military-esque. Over that, she wore a dirty white lab coat, with several scorch marks on it. She appeared to be in her early teens.

"Geez," she grumbled, smacking loudly on her lollipop. "First, you don't show up on time, then you bring way more people than you said you would. Of course, I'm gonna hide behind a spatial distortion camouflage."

"You can't just bust out lost technology at the slightest excuse, nitwit!"

"You're the last person who has any right to scold me! Consider me irate."

Nobody else knew what spatial distortion or lost technology meant, but eventually, the girl realized everyone was staring at her, and she gave them a wave.

"'Sup, I'm Eug. Lena Eug. Dr. Eug is fine! I'm technically the king of the dwarves, so, you know, respect that."

"Th-the king of the dwarves?! Seriously?!"

"Mm, in name alone! I was gonna abdicate eventually but I'm still the unrivaled number one in craftsmanship, refining, and invention, so I can't quit no matter how much I want to. Before I knew it, I was a hundred-something old-timer!"

Eug snapped the sucker against her teeth, and the group was stunned into silence again. People said they were thirty-something all the time, but you didn't get many people living long enough to coin a word for their second century.

"Master's not the only one...," Marie whispered.

Eug's ears caught this, and she was instantly inches from her, closing the distance in the blink of an eye like a martial arts master.

"Please don't lump me in with her! Consider me aghast."

Marie yelped, nearly falling over. "No, no," she protested. "The way you just moved is definitely in the same wheelhouse!"

"Physically speaking, I may be a bit stronger than your average person, but I'm enhancing that effect with these!"

Eug lifted her feet, showing off her boots as if she were bragging about her new sneakers.

"I can only move that fast because these boosts have a repulsion regulation dial built in! My own invention! They let me run real fast or leap giant trees in a single bound! Perfect for everyday wear!"

"You don't need to jump over trees every day...," Marie argued.

"I thought you'd say that!" Eug said, grinning. She pointed her

lollipop at the witch. "But it's not exactly true if you're staying in Kunlun—which I am. They see my hands idle for a second, they expect me to pitch in, and without these, I'd never keep up!"

"We don't 'expect' a thing!" Alka corrected, shaking her head. "She's just always been uncomfortable with being in anyone's debt."

"Sure am! And once I accept a job or research project, I can't sit still until it's cleared away. You know that, too, Alka."

"Such a perfectionist."

Eug just grinned, clearly enjoying Alka's reactions. She popped the sucker out of her mouth and pointed it at Vritra this time.

"Vri, baby," she cooed.

The belt flinched, but Eug ignored this.

"You're the guardian beast, but you were wandering the wilds outside Kunlun? That really stuck a wrench in my plans."

"What plans are those?! And the root cause is entirely Alka's..."

Eug's boots launched off the ground, closing the gap. She grabbed a fistful of Vritra, glaring at him.

"Like I said, Alka is the embodiment of idiocy, the root of all evil, prone to disrupting everything on a whim carried too far! I told *you* to guard Kunlun with that fact seared deep into your collective unconsciousness!"

Even Alka got indignant at this one.

"Back up, Eug!" she said. "The embodiment of *what*? I can't let that go unchallenged!"

Vritra quickly tried to redirect Eug's rage.

"Exactly!" he barked. "Why would you want to make an apron out of my hide?! Beyond insulting! The hide of any roaming dragon would have sufficed!"

The idea of a roaming dragon horrified the bystanders, but everyone *in* the argument failed to notice.

"Mm?" Alka said, as if she'd just remembered something. "Wasn't that apron your idea, Eug? You said it would be a great present for Lloyd, super durable, last him a lifetime."

There was a long silence.

"But I digress!" Eug exclaimed. "Let's all get back to Kunlun, pronto!"

Eug marched off as if nothing at all had happened. Though perhaps she was walking a bit *too* fast.

"You'll answer for this, Eug!" Vritra roared. Then he bobbed his buckle to the others. "I'm sorry, they're always like this."

"I'd heard the stories," Choline assured. "But they really *are* off the charts, Chrome."

"Mm. That aside…how *are* we getting there? The back of this cave is a dead end. It doesn't lead anywhere…"

Chrome knew the local terrain like the back of his hand, so he was particularly baffled.

"Aha! I see," Alka said, stopping just outside the cave.

"What *do* you see?" Selen asked, baffled. "How does this get us to Kunlun?"

Eug smirked at her.

"Excellent question! Allow me to explain. I've applied spatial distortion to this otherwise ordinary cave—the *warp gate* rune!"

"Runes?!" Choline pounced. She was a mage studying runes but had never heard of a warp gate.

"Yes, the lost wisdom of the ancients. If you've heard of them, I gather you're an academic of some kind?" Eug said, as if she were praising a bright child. As she did, she charged some marks on the rock face with magic.

The marks were part of a mural that seemed to depict a person passing through a hole.

"Clever disguise, right? You've gotta be real precise about the destination or who knows where you'll end up. Alka's the wrong choice for that sort of detail. She's the personification of slapdash, after all."

"Slapdash, my foot!" Alka yelled. "Still, given how little magic you have, it's hard to believe you can use runes on this scale."

"I'm a perfectionist, remember? Give me a few days, and this is entirely doable."

This got Marie's interest.

"Why spend all this time making a gate in a cave, though? Is the teleport not an option? What about the world's worst magic spell that lets trouble drop in with no appointment or announcement?"

There was a lot of spite behind this last remark, but, well, given how often Alka showed up out of the blue demanding food or tea or harassing Lloyd, who could blame her?

"Yeah, about that," Eug said. "That teleport crap is something only an off-the-scales inhuman creature like Alka can use. And Alka's gonna be weakened and unable to use her magic for a while, so we figured it was best to secure an alternate route."

"*Inhuman* is certainly the right word for it. Even by that standard, she's off the charts— Wait, she won't be able to use any spells?"

No one was prepared for a weakened Alka.

"I figured she hadn't mentioned it!" Eug shouted. "Witch lady, while we're restoring Vritra, Alka's physical abilities will plummet, and she won't be able to use any magic at all."

This was an astonishing revelation. And the most astonished person...was Alka.

"Huh? Wait, Eug, you never mentioned this!" she yelped, horrified.

"How do *you* not know?" Eug replied, giving her a look of contempt. "The guardian beast of Kunlun—Vritra—is storing *the power* in you. Even just having him stuck in belt form already has your notoriously ludicrous abilities going haywire, right?"

"Oh, right," Alka said. "We wrote it into the ancient script that I could use *the power*."

"Yes." Vritra nodded. "Going from a hideous monster to a belt would disrupt the function of my Words."

"Yup, and restoration will leave you stuck in an egg for a few days, shutting off Alka's power entirely. It's like how virus protection software doesn't function fully while the update's running—same thing."

"……Ancient script? Virus? Up date?" Phyllo muttered. This string of unfamiliar terms was making her head spin.

"Eug!" Alka screeched, preventing her from answering.

"Whoops…uh, pretend I didn't say that."

Eug made a show of licking her lollipop.

"…Geez, well, fine," Alka accepted. "Point taken. I totally forgot."

At this point, Lloyd stepped forward. "I see!" he said, bowing. "Since the chief can't use her teleport, you had to do a lot of work! Thank you so much."

"More or less," Eug acknowledged, nodding. She got back to the task at hand.

"My head hurts already," Marie groaned, slumping over. These people talked about advanced technology (like ancient runes) as if they'd called a carriage for you.

Chrome and Choline were frozen to the spot, in the exact same frame of mind. The grown-ups had had way less exposure to Alka's antics, meaning they were far less equipped to handle this sort of thing.

Eug shot them a sly grin, then held her hand up to the cave entrance. And the back of it vanished, as it had been plunged into water.

The grown-ups gulped, and Eug spun her sucker, looking satisfied.

"See? Here's the entrance."

Riho stepped forward with a sinister grin. "All right! Let's hit this legendary village up!"

"Oh! I can finally meet Lloyd's family!"

"……And people stronger than me."

Riho, Selen, Phyllo (and Marie) had spent enough time with Lloyd and Alka that they didn't even bat an eye at this feat.

Meanwhile, the older two were staring at the warp gate like it was their first encounter with civilization.

"Um…so if we go through that," Chrome said, "we'll be at the furthest reaches of the continent?"

He approached with caution—like a thief sneaking up to a watchdog. Chrome was usually barking orders, so it was rare to see him cringing.

Riho slapped him on the back, as excited as a kid the day before a picnic. Not a pat or even a donk, but a straight-up thwack.

"Don't chicken out now!" she said. "You think you can score any loot with that attitude?"

She had so lost track of their goal here.

"I'm not chickening out!" Chrome roared. "Hey! Don't push! No pushing! I need a moment!"

"Get a move on!" Selen said, helping Riho push. "You're blocking the line! And my love for Lloyd!"

"……She has no notion what this is about, does she?" Vritra muttered. "My mistress is nothing if not consistent."

He may have come to regret possessing her belt. He was definitely trying to mime a wince.

Finally steeling his nerve, Chrome took a deep breath, as if he were about to dive into water, and stepped into the cave.

"Hngg?!" he grunted. A sudden floating sensation had washed over him.

One after another, the rest of the party followed him and found themselves face-to-face with an incredible view.

"Wow…," Riho gasped, speaking for everyone.

A field was covered in flowers, their smell so sweet, everyone wanted to take some home.

They were surrounded by snowcapped mountains that rose so high, it was hard to believe this was the same continent. A river flowed down from those mountains, snowmelt water so clear, you wanted to scoop up a mouthful.

Everyone spread their arms, taking a deep breath.

It felt like airing out the inside of your body.

"Such clean air! Crisp and refreshing!" Riho gushed, feeling amazing. Then she turned to Alka. "So where do we go to find the lucrative monsters?"

Her candor was definitely refreshing! In a sense.

"Uh, Riho, this is just a normal village," Lloyd remarked. "There's no monsters, lucrative or not. My hometown is right over there!"

He pointed at a tiny settlement surrounded by fences.

The larger house at the top of a hill was probably Alka's home. She *was* the chief, after all.

Beyond that, wheat swayed in the fields.

"So pastoral! Exactly the sort of place where you want to spend time with the one you love until death do you part."

That last part sure took on a sinister vibe when Selen said it.

"R-right," Chrome gasped, wiping the sweat from his brow with the back of his hand. "Given the fairy tales, I'd expected something more horrifying, but...mm, pastoral is *way* better."

The village, mountains, and forests all looked totally normal, and this was a huge relief.

Mind you, that forest was filled with treants, a terrifying plant monster. And the fence around the village was made of treant wood. A rare, valuable resource... It was basically like building a barricade out of ivory.

There were definitely signs of outlandishness around, but...nobody noticed.

"This takes me back!" Alka said, grinning at everyone. "I remember when I first brought Marie here... She was so young and innocent."

"It really does *look* normal," Marie emphasized, memories draining all color from her face.

"Princ...I mean, Marie? What's wrong?"

"Oh, Colonel Choline. I...was just remembering how I...may have kicked this horned rabbit..."

"Wow, that could be rough. Hurts if you get stabbed!"

"And I didn't think Kunlun horned rabbits would be eleven yards long and shrouded in lava! I thought it was a boulder, and then I saw the ears…"

Regular horned rabbits were more like eleven inches, and basically the same as normal rabbits—a super-weak target new adventurers used for practice.

Well, in Kunlun, they had horns like drills made for boring through bedrock and wrapped themselves in molten rock found deep below the crust. When they fell asleep, they looked just like boulders with ears, but they'd attack anyone who approached and could easily take out even a veteran adventurer in the blink of an eye.

"…………Ha-ha-ha, no way," Choline said.

"Oh, right," Alka piped up, pointing into the distance. "There's a burrow over that way."

There were a number of huge holes in the rock. Normal horned rabbits burrowed into dirt, only deep enough for your ankles, so people warned kids not to trip over their tunnels. They were almost cute.

But this was more like a mine where all the ore had long since been excavated. These holes were gonna catch a lot more than ankles.

"Those…are their burrows?"

"Yup! No rabbits in them now, but they're like pitfalls. One of you lot fall in, you'll never get out on your own. Even the villagers don't go near the place without good reason, so better look out."

Choline took another look around her, finally realizing there was no telling what was actually a monster.

"But that rabbit was really tender and tasty! The villagers hunt them just like ordinary rabbits," Marie stated, eyes going out of focus.

"You know," Lloyd said, "I don't think I ever saw you here, Marie."

"I was only here for about six months, on the edge of town," she explained, pointing. "Mostly training with Master."

Lloyd was very surprised.

"Really? The chief told me there were terrifying monsters in there, and I should stay away."

"Wha—?" Marie gasped, then turned and glared at Alka.

"I did say that!" Alka chuckled, not the slightest bit guilty. "A boob monster, growing way too fast!"

"What the hell is a boob monster?!"

"Given your situation, I figured it would be better to keep the villagers away. That was my excuse!"

"R-right..."

Marie winced at this.

Her father had fallen into the clutches of a demon lord, and she'd barely escaped Azami with her life. Alka had found her, and while her usual behavior betrayed no trace of this, she actually did think things through sometimes, even if this was literally impossible to tell... Anyway, Marie raised her opinion of Alka slightly.

However...it *was* Alka.

"But it was just an excuse! I knew I had to keep Lloyd as far from you as possible to avoid any unwanted sparks flying."

"I take everything back!" Marie yelled, grabbing a fistful of Alka's shirt.

Alka just grinned at her. "Don't be ridiculous! Why would I let a boob monster like you anywhere near an innocent young man? You'd warp his sexual preferences in the wrong direction! I can't have that! Chance encounters at a young age are just setups for later reunions, and what if he mistakes that for the hand of destiny?! I thwarted that with all my might!"

Alka's perspective wasn't entirely without merit. A boy on the cusp of adolescence coming face-to-face with a pair of very large breasts could give him a permanent preference. It was almost inevitable.

...Not that avoiding this would really increase the odds of him preferring them *small*. Even freshly hatched chicks were unlikely to imprint on an extreme sexual preference like "flat as a cutting board."

"Listen, kid grandma...mm?"

Before Marie could unleash her rage, she saw Selen, Riho, and Phyllo all clapping their hands, sinister smiles on their lips—quietly celebrating Alka's triumph like the blacksuits from a certain famous gambling manga.

""*"Thank* you.*"""

Lloyd's harem would hardly have welcomed a fated reunion with a childhood crush.

Meanwhile, Lloyd was deep in the throes of his typical misunderstanding.

"I see! Marie was training against terrible monsters! That's Azami's secret hero for you!"

By this point, he was basically just wrong about everything Marie did.

Faced with his look of unvarnished admiration, Marie coughed awkwardly and got back to the point.

"Uh, so I only went into the village proper a handful of times…but each of them was…memorable. Oh, look, villagers."

Marie was gazing into the distance. A whole crowd of townsfolk had come out to greet them.

"Oh, Grandpa! And…you all came!"

Lloyd darted off, delighted.

"Lloyd!"

"Welcome back!"

"You look so happy!"

Normal villagers greeting a boy come home. A typical sight was unfolding before everyone's eyes.

Only Riho seemed disgruntled by how normal it all was.

"I mean, they're definitely all as dangerous as Lloyd is…but more normal than I expected?"

When Lloyd first sat down next to her, she'd believed herself in mortal peril, so she sure had come a long way! Or maybe just got used to it.

Chrome was every bit as good as her at detecting strength. His square frame had gone even squarer, and he'd stiffened up like a block of stone ready for carving.

Meanwhile, the martial artist, Phyllo, was fully on guard, sweat running down her brow.

"You hanging in there, Phyllo?"

"...............I feel like I'm standing on a battlefield."

Choline gave her a worried look. Phyllo was standing on the windswept field, on full alert like a scout deep in enemy territory.

Riho shook her head, disappointed.

"Maybe I got my hopes too high...I was expecting houses made of gold and out-of-place artifacts lying in the streets."

Marie gave her a pat on the shoulders.

"............You say that, but...your eyes are about to pop out of your head."

"Seriously? Eye-popping fortunes?"

"Well, if you took a photo, you might be able to sell it for a pretty high price. Look there."

"There?"

She followed Marie's finger. To a perfectly ordinary two-story country house.

A family was chatting outside. Kids were running around.

"Heartwarming pastoral scene, sure," Riho noted. "Some people might call that a priceless treasure, but I'm more looking for—"

But what happened next silenced her.

"Oh, I forgot something upstairs!"

"Oh? I'll get it, Mom!" The kid jumped right in through the second-story window.

"Thanks!"

"...............Come again?"

Residents of reality all made the same strangled grunt.

That child wasn't even five years old but had jumped ten yards. Like someone had dangled a rope out the upstairs window and yanked him up. No one could believe their eyes.

"Ah-ha-ha," Lloyd chuckled, totally not getting why everyone was surprised. "Yeah, country folk don't have the best manners."

He described vaulting to a second-story window the way you would detail closing a door with your feet. No one knew how to respond to this.

Looking closely, villagers were running across roofs, bounding from one to another...

"I do that myself," Lloyd admitted. "Out here, we all run across roofs when we're in a hurry. You can go straight to your destination, but... well, it's a little embarrassing to do when people are looking."

Leave it to Lloyd to treat roofs like a shortcut.

...Kunlun's strangeness was only just beginning to sink its teeth into everyone.

"Oh, look out! Don't stand in the way."

"Huh?"

Alka was pointing at what looked like a bale of hay—the kind you use for target practice. Judging by the condition of it, many an arrow had been fired at it.

"Uh, right," Selen said, but didn't seem sure why.

If this was a target, it wasn't in use—there were no archers in sight.

Selen took a half-step back, still confused...and something flew past her at an alarming speed.

Shunk!

A massive arrow sliced through the air.

"Wha?! Enemy attack?!" Chrome braced himself.

A middle-aged woman came strolling over.

"Oh, my, sorry about that," she apologized.

"...Erm. That's okay..."

The woman unwrapped a piece of paper from the arrow's shaft and looked it over.

"Lesse...," she mumbled. "'*I'll be home in an hour, so make sure dinner's on the table*'? All righty."

Everyone realized the arrow had just been a message.

They looked in the direction it had come from and saw nothing. Just clouds around distant mountain peaks.

"Uh, no way…"

Had someone shot an arrow from that mountain peak and hit this target, just to send a message?

The idea crossed everyone's mind, but they all had a trace of common sense lurking in the corner of their mind, and it instantly dismissed the idea.

No waaay.

But even as they rejected it, the woman wrote a reply.

"I'm making your favorite stewed potatoes…"

She picked up a rock from the ground at her feet and wrapped the paper around it.

"Hup!" She lightly tossed the rock toward the mountains…

Ultrasonic fastball.

The rock shot high into the sky, slicing the very clouds and starting a small avalanche where it hit the snowcapped peak.

While everyone gaped, the woman smiled faintly, looking down at her wrist.

"Oh, dear, I hit the snow! Nothing good comes with age."

"Ah-ha-ha," Lloyd said, stepping in to explain. "Out here in the boonies, we still use old ways to communicate… We don't have phones or magic stones like the army."

He seemed convinced everyone was horrified because this was somehow old-fashioned.

"……No, Master, that's not it," Phyllo assured him. Even *she* was on the sensible side today. Treasure this fleeting moment, dear reader.

Their stupor was interrupted by the raspy voice of an old man.

"Pardon me, travelers. Mind letting me pass?"

"Oh, sorry…er, what the—?!"

Slung over the old man's shoulder…was a cannon. A surreal sight, indeed. A look of fear flashed in their eyes—what crazy shit was gonna happen next?

The man lowered the cannon to the ground with a thud that shook the earth. It must be *really* heavy.

"A-are you going to shoot that at the mountains?" Chrome asked.

The old man looked at him like he was nuts.

"My son forgot his canteen, so I've gotta take it to him!"

"Canteen? Uh…"

The elderly man aimed the cannon at the mountains, then climbed inside. With only his head poking out, he called out to the rock-throwing lady.

"Neighbor, can you charge the magic stone for me?"

"Oh, sure!" She gave him a huge grin, approached, and started doing something.

"Magic? Er…oh!"

There was a magic stone on the side of the cannon, likely an explosive one.

The amount of magic the middle-aged woman poured into it was *bonkers*.

"………That's more magic than either Mena or Rol has," Choline muttered.

No sooner had the words left her mouth than there came a loud explosion, and the old man rocketed off toward the distant mountains.

"Oof, I shoulda put a little more in… Nothing good comes with age."

That…that wasn't enough? Could that elderly guy survive this?! As everyone gaped in horror, Lloyd stepped in to explain once more.

"Here in the boonies, when we want to get to the mountains fast, we all use cannons to fly. But you can't carry much with you because it'll mess up the aim and you'll end up in the wrong place entirely. Also, they just slide all the way down the side of the mountain to get back."

"Oh, um…but that looks pretty perpendicular…"

Normal skiers considered a thirty-degree slant a pretty difficult course. Angles like this weren't really "sliding" so much as skydiving without a parachute.

One shocking sight after another had slowly robbed the Azami contingent of their capacity for speech.

With the gang still reeling from the grandpa cannon, a group of woodcutters shuffled into sight.

Every one of them had the same face, the same clothes, and the same ax.

""""""Don't push yourself, lady."""""""

Oh, and…they all spoke in unison.

"Come on now, merge back together before you come home!"

""""""Oops, sorry."""""""

With this helpful reminder, one woodcutter raised his hand, said, "Release!" and his clones vanished in a series of smoke clouds. The one remaining logger shouldered his bundle of wood again.

"Whew… Oh, Lloyd! Welcome back!"

"Woodcutter! It's been ages, huh?"

When Lloyd ran over to him, there was another puff of smoke, leaving a log where the man had been.

"Ah!"

"…Heh-heh-heh, still can't see through that one, huh?"

The woodcutter appeared behind Lloyd, emerging from his shadow, and clapped him on the shoulder.

"If you were a treant, you'd be lumber by now, Lloyd!"

"Argh, come on!"

"Fooled again! I bet there's nobody in the city using proper tree-felling techniques! You *would* get out of practice, ha-ha-ha."

Everyone thought the same thing.

This wasn't a lumberjack. He was a ninja—just like the legends said.

At the least, he had to be using ninja-like techniques…

None of the ordinary humans could keep their jaws closed.

"…I take it back," Riho croaked. "Nothing normal here."

"R-Riho! L-look!" Selen yelped, pointing across the street.

There…was a fish monster! A killer piranha!

Everyone grabbed their weapons…but something seemed fishy here.

The tyrant of the depths was floating belly up with its eyes rolled back.

Beneath it, carrying the killer piranha, was Lloyd's grandpa Pyrid. Judging by the beads of water dripping from what remained of his hair, he'd just dived in to catch it.

They'd all lost count of how many surprises they'd had that day.

"Hello, everyone!" Pyrid boomed with a pleasant smile. "We'll be having this for dinner tonight! C'mon, Chief, show everyone around."

"Working on it, Pyrid. Get moving, people, get over the culture shock, and let's head for my house."

Did this even count as culture shock? They all questioned that concept…

Except for Phyllo. A whole different set of emotions banished that thought from her mind.

"………Heh-heh."

The moment she saw Pyrid carrying the killer piranha, her aura changed completely. Her lips twisted into a rare smile.

"Phyllo?" Selen squeaked. "What's wrong? Why are you so weirdly happy?"

The two had been going to school together long enough that this was actually the biggest curiosity of the day. Phyllo smiling was enough to surpass all Kunlun legends.

Phyllo slid one foot forward, shifting her weight so she could attack at any time.

"Mm? What's up, girlie?" Pyrid said.

In that instant, it was like there was a line in the sand between the two of them.

If either crossed it, a battle would start—like the border between two countries in conflict.

"…Pyrid the Fierce God, I believe. May I request instruction?"

Phyllo raised her hands. When he saw her stance, Pyrid smiled, like it brought back memories.

"Oh? Oh! That's the stance from the martial arts style I founded! No one could handle the training, and I was forced to close the place in tears."

"…Training by dropping off a cliff to shatter boulders was certainly punishing."

"Basic defensive skills."

"Gh! ………that was *basic*?"

"I never manage to teach beyond the fundamentals… These days, the villagers use those as simple workouts or morning calisthenics."

"…Seriously, Master?" Phyllo turned to Lloyd with an uncharacteristic yelp.

"Uh, yes. Grandpa thought up some healthy exercises for the whole village. How is it you know them, Phyllo?"

The legendary style left by the Fierce God Pyrid.

Phyllo had absorbed that training, honing her body beyond that of mere mortals.

It was the core of her identity—and it was being treated like pre-workout stretches. Uh-oh, her eyes just rolled back in her head. She was totally breaking character now.

"Interesting girl." Pyrid chuckled. "Been a while since I got a formal request for instruction! Gimme a second, though. I gotta toss this fish in the kitchen."

Riho instantly appeared next to him, rubbing her hands like a craft merchant.

"I'll help carry that thing! I'd love to help! Please let me help."

"Oh, how nice of you…cat-eyed girl."

Evidently, Phyllo wasn't the only one whose emotions overcame all other thoughts.

Naturally, in Riho's case, she wasn't being nice—she was out for profit. Her plot was to peel off some scales from this high-level monster to sell later.

Her eyes morphed into the shape of gold coins. Riho hefted the killer piranha like precious cargo.

Phyllo must have assumed she was doing this for her because she smiled faintly and said, "......Thanks, Riho."

"Pfft, whatever. We're friends!"

A magnanimous gesture, but those eyes were still gold coins... She was so transparent that you couldn't really call her a liar.

Oblivious to that, Phyllo beckoned Pyrid to the town square.

"Pyrid," Alka said. "She's our guest. Careful with her."

"Don't worry. I'm not as bad as you. I'll just put her through some basic kata sequences, fit for any martial artist."

"Just that, huh? Well, Phyllo can probably handle it. Long as you don't do anything fatal, we can always heal her later."

And with that terrifying remark, Alka waved everyone toward her house.

Alka's house stood on the top of the hill.

She led them to a room with a view of the wheat fields.

There stood a set of legless chairs made of bamboo and linen—a common choice in the boonies when the weather was nice, but only Lloyd and Eug seemed comfortable. Everyone else entered the room like they might have hidden traps—like if you opened a drawer, it might explode.

Alka plopped herself down in the chair at the head of the seating arrangement.

"Relax, people!" she said.

"Uh, Master...that's a tall order."

After all the surprises, everyone was on edge. Selen was studiously whispering, "I've gotta get used to it somehow...," but that was probably the best any of them could manage right now.

A plump woman—who seemed like Alka's housekeeper—took the killer piranha from Riho, waving them all toward the seats.

"Thanks for coming so far... Chief, we finished cleaning up."

"Well done. If you could be so kind as to bring us tea?"

"Oh, where are my manners? I'll bring it right away!" She hustled off to the kitchen. Riho tried to follow.

"Let me help!"

"Thanks so much!"

"Not at all!"

Riho wasn't being helpful or anything. She just figured this would help her harvest killer piranha parts. Those eyes weren't going back to normal anytime soon. Major greed, indeed.

"That Riho kid is going places!" Eug said, watching Riho smoothly worm her way into the kitchen. "Boundless curiosity and hustle—even if it's all for money, I respect it."

Then she sat up, getting down to business.

"I wanna start Vritra's revival right away, but...you all look exhausted."

"Uh, yeah...," Marie said wearily. If the sole person who had visited Kunlun in the past was in this state...everyone else had probably shed a few pounds.

"I need to make preparations, so let's do it tomorrow," Eug suggested.

"That'll work just fine!" Alka agreed. "You came all this way. Kick back and have fun!"

Selen's expression immediately brightened.

"Sleepover! I get to be under the same roof as Lloyd! In the same bed!"

Being in her crush's hometown had Selen at max enthusiasm. Despite the three-digit age difference, Alka's love for Lloyd was just as strong, and she wasn't about to let *that* happen.

"Please! You think I'd allow your shenanigans?!"

She was seated at the head of the circle and, for once, actually seemed like a village chief.

"S-sorry," Selen mumbled, cowed.

"That pleasure is mine alone!"

Never mind. Chief's chair or not, Alka was Alka.

Riho and the housekeeper emerged from the kitchen, bearing tea. "She up to this again?" the lady said. "I do apologize. She's been like this since Lloyd was a child. Took the whole village watching her to make sure no crimes went down."

Everyone turned and glared at the kid grandma. There's an old expression that goes, "A leopard never changes its spots." Fitting for a predator.

Their glares were fierce enough that even Alka grew uncomfortable.

"Ahem," she coughed. "These guests will be staying here tonight. Can you get rooms ready for them?"

"Oh! We'll have to get the futons out. Where did I put those?"

The housekeeper put her hand on her chin, thinking. Finally, she remembered.

"Oh, that's right! When Merthophan arrived, I dragged them out of the back room."

Merthophan.

That name got Choline up on one knee, looking grim.

"Oh, where's Merthophan at?" Alka asked.

"Still in the fields. He's a hard worker!"

"E-excuse me!" Choline said, jumping in. "Would it be possible for me to see him?"

She seemed flustered. Next to her, Chrome bowed his head as well.

"I'd appreciate it if you could point us in the right direction."

Catching on, Alka smirked. "How sweet," she said. "He should be working the fields 'round back today. Can't see him from here, but he should be right over that hill."

"Sorry, I'm just gonna go see!" Choline ran out of the room, yanking on her boots. Chrome bowed and followed after her.

"Merthophan wound up here?" Riho asked, handing out teacups.

"Sounds like Abaddon charmed him and put him up to all manner of things. He's working the fields here to pay for his sins. Should be pretty well cleansed by now."

Alka glanced at Marie.

Looking grim, Marie took a sip of tea…like she was swallowing the last traces of resentment.

"Yeah, I suppose so. In a weird way, he did lead me to meet you, Master…and Lloyd."

"Huh?" Lloyd said, confused. "Why are you the one forgiving him, Marie? And this is Colonel Merthophan? The drunk?"

Marie just smiled, happy to have met him.

Just then, two village children came stomping into the house. They must have been playing outside because their hands and knees were covered in dirt.

"Hey! Don't track mud into the house!"

The children ignored the fussy housekeeper, making a beeline for Alka.

"What's the rush?" she said, smiling at them.

"Chief! Hurry!"

"A monster!"

Riho's eyes flashed, and she dove in.

"Really? Where?"

"Over there!"

"Oh no!" Riho exclaimed. "We'll go on ahead and slow it down!"

Riho sprinted off, the children leading the way.

"Oh, dear… No need to make such a fuss. Well, her heart's in the right place, at least."

It wasn't.

She was just hoping to pick up the scraps left once the high-level monster got taken out.

Everyone watched her go.

"…She's forgotten this is Kunlun," Alka muttered with a sigh. "It won't be an ordinary monster…"

Donning her military uniform boots mid-run, Choline left the chief's house, heading around back.

It was hardly harvest season, but for some reason, all the wheat was a lovely golden shade.

She ran through the fields like a startled rabbit.

Merthophan's here!

A sullen former colleague she spent a lot of time working with.

A poor soul, so concerned for the state of his country, his mind had been captured by a demon lord.

And…the man of Choline's affections.

I don't have the slightest clue what to say to him, but…

Maybe she'd chew him out, maybe she'd punch him, maybe she'd just start crying.

He just disappeared on me… And I have to see him again!

Lloyd's power had freed him, and Merthophan had come here to atone—and Choline had come here to see him.

Out of breath, she reached the back of the fields, by the vast forest. There, Choline stopped, squinting at the wheat around her.

Golden waves shimmered in the sunlight.

And a silver head moved through the sea of gold.

"Geez, you run off like that," Chrome gasped, catching up with her. Then he saw the same thing. "Mm? Is that…?"

©Nao Watanuki

"Merthophan! Yo, Merthophan!"

At the sound of his name, the silver head shot up and turned toward them.

A familiar, powerful voice rang out.

"I know that voice... Another of the chief's schemes?"

The silver-haired man approached Choline, and the wheat parted...

Merthophan wore a cloth around his neck, held a hoe in one hand, and had a loincloth around his waist.

"Right then... Oh, Choline, nice to see you. You too, Chrome."

His loincloth was a little out of place, so he casually adjusted it. Perhaps it was pulling on his crotch funny.

Choline stood face-to-face with the kind of man so absorbed in field-work, he no longer cared for his appearance, wearing the kind of outfit that could kill the love of the century...

"H-hi there...Merthophan."

Well, she managed to speak, at least. Just barely hanging on to the scraps of her affection.

Merthophan adjusted the seat of his loincloth like a girl in a bikini on the beach.

"Mm," he grunted.

He was always a man of few words.

"Looks like you haven't changed much inside, Merthophan."

Chrome put a lot of stress on the word *inside,* but Merthophan didn't notice.

"No, I have. With all the crazy stuff that goes on here—it takes a lot to surprise me now."

They were getting a glimpse of crazy right now, but they were forced to accept that the loincloth was just a thing now. Both managed a strained smile.

"Well, that'd do it!" Choline said. "If they're always like this..."

"Let's sit down in the shade," Merthophan suggested and led them to the base of a nearby tree.

Birds were chirping. Warm sunlight and the smell of the earth helped Choline and Chrome recover.

"Surprised you two came all the way here," Merthophan admitted, wiping the sweat from his brow.

"Yeah, we were surprised, too…by your outfit…"

Oh, they were specifically calling him out on the loincloth thing now.

Merthophan looked hurt.

"That's hardly worth being surprised about. I know, when I was a soldier, I was always in uniform. But now I'm carrying a hoe in the fields and dressed for that kind of work. That's all."

Not many farmers went loincloth only, really. Merthophan ignored their stares, wiping his face with the cloth.

"You're pretty tan, there."

"Yeah, once I got to Kunlun, I was put in charge of the wheat fields. Lately, I've been branching out to other crops. Farming has a lot of depth. The more time you put into it, the better everything grows."

"Like military cadets?"

"Yeah, but the crops don't argue back…and I kinda miss that. How's your new crop doing?"

Merthophan finally asked about the cadets, about Azami.

He still loved his country. That part of him hadn't changed.

"They're arguing back, for sure. A constant struggle! I miss running that cafeteria. The other day…"

Merthophan listened to Chrome grumble with a smile.

Choline waited for Chrome to get it off his chest, fidgeting.

Despite the love-slaying fashion choice, she'd managed to cling to her crush, but it had been so long, she just wasn't sure what to say, or how to engage.

This wasn't like her, and eventually, Chrome noticed and shot Merthophan a look.

"Mm?"

Merthophan gave her a long, searching look. Then he smiled.

"Choline, I know I'm making things more difficult than they need to be. And I'm sorry."

"O-oh, I didn't… Y-you know me…I never was one to…"

When she started fidgeting even harder, Merthophan pointed into the brush.

"You need to go? The earth in Kunlun is so rich that you can plow the fields and not need much fertilizer, so we don't really collect waste anywhere. Number one or number two, just go on the side of the field, it's all good. I'm certainly grateful for the offer of fresh manure, but…"

"Drop deeeeeead!"

Choline's right hook exploded against the loincloth man's solar plexus.

"Gahhhhh!"

Merthophan's death screams echoed across the field.

This was a statement that could take the love of the century, the love of the millennium, and the love of all time and instantly turn that fever down to absolute zero, and it took Choline from shrinking maiden mode back to her usual self.

"Chrome, he's no good," she snapped. "That same military patriot brain has simply swapped genres to agriculture."

"That was definitely your fault, Merthophan."

Merthophan stopped rolling around in pain, staggered to his feet, adjusted the loincloth wedgie. "How so?! I merely stated the facts! Human waste is excellent fertilizer! And this village doesn't have any septic tank–like sanctuary!"

"You owe Choline *and* the word *sanctuary* an apology," Chrome growled.

"I don't get it," Merthophan said but bowed his head anyway. "Sorry, Choline."

"You don't get it?! Arghhhh, why did I ever fall for this guy? Chasing him all the way out here to the boonies only to have it blow up in my face!"

Seriously.

Loincloth Merthophan stayed as oblivious to her affection as he had been when they first met, and as he likely would remain for all of time.

"Hmm, so what *does* bring you all here?" he asked. "I assume the chief put you up to it, but…"

Just then…there was a scream so horrifying, it sounded like the end of the world. Choline and Chrome both flinched.

"Wh-what was that guttural roar?!"

"That was insanely loud!"

The reverb from the cry had sent ripples through the waves of grain.

"Oh," Merthophan said. "That would be a monster."

"A monster?! What *kind* of monster?! Nothing that guttural can be a normal-ass monster! This is something way—!"

"It's a monster!" Merthophan insisted, interrupting her. "No matter what anyone else says!"

"Uh, Merthophan?"

Merthophan looked gravely in the direction of the roaring—so stressed out, he had a tight grip on the fabric of his loincloth. If he pulled any harder, it would all come spilling out.

"Yes, a monster…to the villagers here."

"And that means…?"

Merthophan nodded. He then tied his towel around his head like he was donning a helmet and adjusted his little cloth.

"Come, see for yourselves. The villagers may call it a monster…but it's a demon lord."

Shortly before Choline and Merthophan's upsetting reunion…Riho was sitting on her knees on a path through the rice fields.

How did I get here?

Her expression tinged with regret, she glanced at the sight in front of her.

There stood a man in an elegant white robe.

With two horns on his head.

He was introducing himself.

"Let me say it again. I am the demon lord, Satan."

"R-right."

If someone had said that to Riho on the street, she'd just walk the hell on, but her experience meant she immediately knew exactly how powerful this guy was.

One false move, and I'm dead...

In a town where even killer piranha were just food, something even the villagers called a monster...well, Riho had assumed even a fragment of the spoils would be enough to buy a house.

She'd come running out here, ready to make it rich.

But this was the reality. She was overcome with remorse.

Yeah, they treat normal monsters like fish or game! Of course, anything they actually call a monster is gonna be mad dangerous! Am I an idiot?!

Definitely. If we want to give her an excuse, the children who reported it sure didn't make it sound that bad. The way they talked, it was like they'd just found a really big frog.

Oblivious to her shame, Satan was launching into a lecture on how mankind's relentless pursuit of energy was violating the natural order, sounding more like a radical college professor than a demon lord.

"If human overpopulation continues, the sea levels will rise! Half the land will sink into the ocean!"

"Huh..."

"I cannot allow frail humans to control this land through sheer numbers!"

Getting a serious talk from a demon lord was a special kind of torture. Like how laymen feel anytime a politician launches into a passionate explanation of wonky policy details.

Riho was busy deflecting the demon lord's lecture on human anni-hilation by rotating through, "Uh-huh," "Yeah," "I agree," and "Oh?" This can be startlingly effective, so by all means, try it at home.

"You're quite promising for a human. Well? Care to become my min-ion? Work hard enough, and half this land could be yours!"

Deploying her best listening skills to buy time seemed to have cur-ried a disturbing amount of favor.

This guy's an idiot.

"Well, if you don't work hard enough, half the land will be gone any-way! Ha-ha-ha! That's a satanic joke! Get it?"

Satan doubled over laughing, but it wasn't at all clear what part of that was supposed to be funny.

Someone come quick... I dunno if I can take much more of this...

The demon lord's raw strength was bad enough, but handling a one-on-one discussion with anyone who lacked conversation skills was *really* rough. As awkward as being stuck in an elevator with someone you *sorta* know.

Then someone gray-rocked their conversation.

Thud.

That wasn't a metaphor. It was a literal rock.

"Wh-what? A rock?" Satan barked, blinking at the thing beneath his feet.

One of those children had thrown it at him.

"Aw, I missed!"

"You suck!"

Apparently, they'd been so busy gathering rocks, they'd only just arrived. They had a big pile of them around their feet, taking turns hurling them at the monster.

"Don't do that, kids!" Riho shrieked. This was a demon lord! If they angered it, Riho could well say good-bye to half her body!

Meanwhile, the demon lord seemed unable to believe anyone would dare throw a rock at him, so he just gaped at the children.

"Don't don't dooooooon't!" Riho wailed, like a dramatic musical sting.

Thud, thud...thunk.

A rock finally hit him. The children shrieked with delight.

Enraged, the demon lord yelled, "You little brats!"

"Eeek!"

The children ignored him, moving on to their next game.

"Whoever breaks those horns wins!"

"You're on!"

A moment later...

Whoosh. A rock shot past the demon lord, making the wind whistle—clearly a much harder throw than what came before.

The rock hit the dirt behind him, sending up a cloud of dust like the splash after a botched dive.

Dirt rained down on Riho like an explosive shell detonating overhead.

Riho and Satan exchanged a look.

"...You know these kids?"

"Sorry, I'm as lost as you are."

This brief interaction was soon ended by a bunch more stones.

Less "thrown" than "launched from a cannon."

Rocks fired one after another, without a second's pause, with peals of laughter as background music.

The dirt raining down at them made it impossible to see a thing. Riho and the demon lord screamed as one.

"Wh-what's even happening?!"

And finally, a rock hit a horn. The demon lord's head snapped back. Whiplash assured. A human would have been hauled straight to the orthopedic clinic.

Instead, the broken tip of the horn went sailing off toward the horizon.

"Wh-wh...why, you little... Aughhhhh!"

Before he could even start yelling at the kids, a rock landed on his other horn. This time, it put a spin on his skull, and that dragged his body with it, sending him twirling through the air until he landed headfirst in a rice paddy.

The kids gave each other a high five.

"Yes! Break damage!"

"And artistic points on that landing!"

Were they scoring a figure-skating match?

Brushing dirt off herself, Riho started scolding the kids.

"H-hey! You can't do that! What if he gets mad and comes after you?"

"That *always* happens," one kid assured her.

"Don't worry, metal arm lady!"

"The first form is no big whoop."

To these kids, the first form of a demon lord really *was* about as threatening as a really big frog.

But this was dire news to Riho's ears. There was more to this fight? She shuddered.

"There's a second form?! That's horrifying!"

As if answering a request, Satan's body started changing color, getting larger.

"So you wish to see my true form?! You will soon know real fear! You'll live just long enough to regret…**being born!**"

His voice rose into a shriek, but the children just cheered.

"Yes! We did it!"

"Eeek! He's so scary!"

They ran off like they'd just rung the doorbell to prank an intimidating old neighbor.

"Uh…no, wait, you're gonna run now?! Who's gonna handle this mess?!"

"Mankind's power has grown too great! If nothing is done, the world has no future!"

"You said humans were 'frail' before, though."

The demon lord was too preoccupied to care about plot holes.

Pitch-black wings unfurled, massive fangs gnashed, muscles bulged, and the demon lord's frame blocked the setting sun.

"Mere rocks can no longer harm me! The Demon Lord Satan cannot be bested by puny projectiles!"

The demon lord's roar echoed.

"Oh, crap, oh, crap... Huh?"

Something rocketed across the sky.

At first, Riho thought there was just something in her eye, but the shape of it soon became clear.

A lump of stone shrouded in flames from the atmospheric friction.

A meteorite falling from space.

"A-a shooting star?!" Riho gasped, like a heroine in a romance manga.

"Hmph!" the demon lord grunted. **"Wishes won't save you now. The extinction of the human race is only a matter of— Huh?"**

Tough luck there, Demon Lord. You're the one going extinct.

The meteorite came in diagonally from over Riho's right shoulder, crashing into the demon lord with all the force of a car accident, sending the monster flying off toward the sunset on the horizon.

"That's a meteorite, not a thrown rock! It doesn't count!"

The demon lord's death throes were a pedantic quibble, but the roar of the meteorite itself drowned them out.

Riho was left on her knees, gaping at the wreckage.

And then the person who'd brought the meteorite down stepped out from behind her.

"Geez, you ran out all excited—good thing, it was such a puny demon lord. I was able to use a comparatively controllable tiny meteorite."

It was Alka. The haze of magic around her hand came from the rune she'd used.

"I like her!" Eug said, snapping her lollipop. "She's true to herself and not afraid to get pushy."

"Are you okay, Riho?" Lloyd asked, running up, the others in tow. "Oh, of course you *would* be. You can handle this stuff better than I ever could. You bought time until the chief could get here!"

Lloyd's concern seemed to have resolved itself. His low self-esteem was just a given at this point.

"N-no, I didn't...," Riho spluttered.

She tried to get up, but her legs gave out, and she wound up grabbing on to Lloyd.

The kids from earlier came running up.

"We played with the metal arm lady!"

"Yeah!"

That wasn't a gaaaaame! Riho felt the tears welling up.

Alka was already scolding the kids. "I told you this before! You can't just play with any old monster!"

"Ugh, it was fine! We're not weak like Lloyd!"

Lloyd winced at this.

"Ah-ha-ha, that's embarrassing. Yeah, even the kids here treat me like this."

"Uh...huh..."

With him looking sheepish inches away from her, Riho started blushing, too.

Selen instantly pried them apart, like a soccer ref about to hand out a red card.

"Okay, okay, okay, hands off Lloyd! Riho! Why are you hanging off him?!"

"M-my knees buckled out from under me!"

"Then my belt will hold you up! *Tightly.*"

"Hey! Not around the neck!"

The same old squabbles, just in a field instead of a classroom.

A bizarre figure stepped in.

"I know there was a demon-monster attack, but that's no excuse for wrecking my farmland! Who did this?! Oh, is that you, Riho Flavin?"

"Who the hell are— Er...Colonel?"

It took her a good ten seconds to realize this hoe-wielding loincloth man was Colonel Merthophan.

"Apologize to the man, kids."

"Uncle Loin—I mean, Merthophan, sorry."

"Uncle Loinclo—I mean, we were throwing rocks to play with the monster."

Apparently, the kids all called him Uncle Loincloth behind his back. The man in question paid this no attention, ruffling the kids' hair.

"These fields are important! Don't do that next time."

"Yes," Alka said, stepping in with the utmost dignity. "If I catch you causing trouble, I'll make you both wear waistcloths, too."

"I won't do it again! I promise!"

"I swear I'll never throw another rock ever again!"

They looked genuinely terrified.

Seeing their reactions, Chrome and Choline clutched their foreheads.

"Who *would* want to dress like that?"

"It is nothing but punishment."

"Don't be ridiculous! This garment is perfect for muddy fieldwork! Easy to move, and so simple to wash later! There is no downside."

Even Kunlun villagers didn't work the farmland in loincloths. Merthophan's intense work wear discourse was falling entirely on deaf ears.

As more villagers gathered, the housekeeper spoke up.

"Oh my, Merthophan! Do you know these people?"

"Yes," he admitted with a relaxed smile, like he was remembering good times. "We were not together long, but they were all excellent students of mine."

With his loincloth digging in between both cheeks, nobody wanted to be referred to as his student. Everyone made a face.

"I feel like they'll take that in entirely the wrong light, so let's just say we're total strangers instead."

"Riho Flavin, I know we had our differences, and I don't blame you for holding that against me."

"Yeah, no, let's pretend we're total strangers. I don't wanna make it sound like we ever had anything in common."

They sounded like a comedy duo splitting up over creative differences. Merthophan was definitely heading off for a low-brow solo career.

"We'd better get back to the house!" Eug suggested. She turned to Riho. "Riho, was it? You need a bath."

"Oh my!" the housekeeper gasped and led the way. "The children make such a fuss over the monsters!" she said. "I hope they weren't too much of a bother. This is just every day here!"

It was? Everyone looked grim.

"You mean something like that shows up once a day?" Marie gasped.

Alka grinned at her. "Not just once! Some days, we'll get three!"

"Three demon lords a day...?" Chrome whispered.

With that note of horror, they headed back to Alka's house.

As darkness fell, the hearth fire lit the room in Alka's home in Kunlun village.

A massive party was getting underway in the main hall. The floor was covered in legless chairs and low tables laden with food.

"We use this for village meetings, but it doubles as a party venue when we got something to celebrate, like today!"

Alka was sitting cross-legged at the head of the room, drooling at the food as it came out. This made her look like the birthday girl, but her true age was referred to in vague terms like *grandma* and *mystery entity*.

"Party-shmarty! They're your guests, but you ain't lifting a finger!" Pyrid scolded.

Pyrid had raised Lloyd and was one of the village leaders. He wasn't pleased with Alka's laziness.

Marie had never seen anyone scold Alka successfully before. She was usually the one getting scolded.

"Such a glorious sight," she mused. "I'm glad I came here."

"Hngg, you'll pay for that when we're back in Azami," Alka growled.

"Don't be ridiculous, Chief!" her housekeeper said. "You're the chief here! We can't have you running off whenever you like! You need to pay for your misdeeds, and the first step is to get up and help!"

"Hngg..." Grumbling, Alka began helping set the tables.

Then Riho came in, face still flushed from the bath.

"'Sup...man, that was a nightmare!"

"Oh, Riho! Not often you wear a skirt."

Riho had her hair down and had a long skirt on—this changed her vibe enough that it had taken them a second to recognize her. She'd gone from looking like a bandit to looking like a nice village girl.

"Yeah, if I'd known this would happen, I'd have brought a change of clothes. I'm even borrowing underwear! And here I thought I could go a day without."

Yeah, she still didn't talk like a nice village girl, and that mithril arm definitely didn't fit that image.

"Honestly, Riho." Selen clucked. "You have no concept of daintiness."

Even as she spoke, there was a rumble—from Phyllo's belly.

"...I'm hungry," Phyllo explained, her expression never changing.

"Geez, I know you can't stop the rumbling, but you could at least look ashamed!"

"...Well, I was in a battle for my life."

Phyllo was covered in small scratches.

And she looked extra honed, like she'd just come back from a hermitage.

"Oh, Phyllo!" Pyrid boomed, patting her on the shoulder. "Sorry I could only run you through a few simple kata! I'll do some proper training with you later, I promise!"

"Those were *kata*?!" Phyllo yelped, altogether discarding her stoic, silent-type routine. She looked utterly astounded. "Kata?! Just kataaaaaaaa?!"

"Ph-Phyllo? Y-you've abandoned your personality!"

Pyrid just laughed. "Such an animated young girl!" he observed.

Not an impression of her anyone in Azami would have. Those who knew her just silently blamed Kunlun.

While this was going on, the food was finally all laid out. Lloyd had been helping set the tables, excited to be back home.

"It's been so long since I've gotten a chance to cook country ingredients! It was a lot of fun!"

"Yeah, well...killer piranha..."

Nothing that high level was gonna show up in the city marketplace. You might call it a delicacy or a hometown specialty, but it definitely outclassed both those terms. It was more like saying tonight's dinner was tyrannosaurus steak.

As Marie winced, Merthophan laid her food in front of her. He had a cook's apron on now.

He was the man who'd tried to take over the country, and she was the princess.

He was the first to break the awkward silence.

"I'd like to formally apologize for my previous misdeeds later tonight. To you, and to Chrome and Choline, and...all your friends."

"Sounds good," Marie said, relaxing. "For now, this is Lloyd's homecoming party. That stuff can wait for later."

Then Alka clapped her hands, drawing everyone's attention.

"The whole village is here, so let's have a toast! Silence, please!"

She stepped into the center of the room, raising a glass.

"Thank you all for coming to my wedding with Lloyd—"

"Chief, you've done that gag before!"

"I know! And I'm not joking! This is serious!"

Yeah, it wasn't really funny. But it also couldn't be taken seriously.

Ignoring Alka's protests, Pyrid stood up and took over the toast. He did this so smoothly, it was like he was actually running a wedding.

"Lloyd's come back home a soldier and brought good friends with him. Glasses up!"

""""Cheers!"""""

With that, the room filled with merriment. For once, it really did seem like a normal village.

The contingent from Azami were gaping at the feast laid out before them.

"This really *is* the kinda food you get at a wedding…"

Chrome and Choline were licking their lips as Merthophan served them.

"Merthophan, you've become a real cook!"

"Yeah! This gizzard skewer's off the charts! You do something special at the prep stage?"

"Nope, just let the natural quality of the ingredients shine," Merthophan said, plating their food.

"The natural quality? Well spoken!"

"I'm not being modest; it really is better stuff…" Without batting an eye, Merthophan launched into a spiel about the ingredients. "I mean, these gizzards come from a chicken—I mean, a basilisk I strangled myself this morning."

""" …… """

Chrome and Choline both dropped their skewers.

A basilisk. A terrifying monster with poisonous breath that could turn you to stone and shatter you… The head and torso were indeed chicken-like, but the back half supposedly went full reptile, turning into a snake's tail.

A single one of them could wipe out an entire town. Defeating one was an epic feat. Nobody would ever consider *eating* it.

"That does leave us without any tail meat," Merthophan explained, heedless of their horror. "The snake part just isn't worth eating, I'm afraid. But the heart is extra tasty! It keeps beating even after you strangle the thing, which does make it a pain to prepare."

As their old friend spoke, Chrome and Choline grew increasingly grave. Apparently, basilisk gizzards were exquisite, offering a flavor beyond that found in any nonpetrifying creatures.

Every member of the Azami contingent thought the same thing: *High-level monsters are treated like poultry!*

They all stopped eating, afraid that what they next touched would be something even more insane.

"…You could build a house with this meal…"

"Don't say it, Phyllo!"

It definitely did taste good, but who could stay hungry if they knew each bite was worth a gold coin?

Regardless of their consternation, dish after dish was spread out on the table. Each accompanied by Merthophan's generous commentary.

"This is excellent," he said, presenting the next dish.

It was roasted onions in a *shutou* sauce. The onions were halved, skin and all, piping hot, served in a fancy dish made from their own crisped skins.

And the *shutou*—a savory squid-based sauce—had a rich odor that tantalized the nostrils.

Once again, they all hesitated to try a bite.

"Don't worry. These are normal onions I personally grew in the fields here."

Riho looked relieved to hear it.

"G-good! Something safe to eat. Obviously, this isn't *all* made from monsters!"

Since this wasn't prepared from high-level drops, Riho happily took a bite.

"Oh, that's good!" she praised. "Piping hot! And the sauce is crazy!"

"This is delicious!" Selen said.

"……Mm."

It was so scrumptious that it immediately reduced their vocabularies. If they'd been food critics on a TV show, the director would have slapped all three of them.

Merthophan grinned happily. Then he got a look like he forgot something, and he turned to Alka.

©Nao Watanuki

"The sauce really pulls the dish together. What was in it, Chief? Squid?"

"Kraken."

"Riiiight, there were ships going missing in the waters between Azami and Rokujou! Investigations couldn't find a cause, but more than a dozen ships had gone AWOL between the two countries. People thought it was pirates or something, and it became a huge international issue...but the real cause makes a great sauce if you strain it!"

"I don't think I can eat any more..."

Smothering international issues with hot onions was not exactly an appetizing proposition.

"Now, now, I went to all the trouble of hunting the thing. Eat up!"

"You caught it, Master?!" Marie wailed.

Alka puffed up her chest, snorting proudly. "Yup! I was just taking a stroll across the ocean, and the thing popped up and sprayed ink at me."

"A stroll...on the ocean?"

"Walking on water is how ladies pass the time."

The ordinary humans pictured Alka walking on water, no land in sight, like she was on the beach. They were at a loss for words.

The less ordinary Kunlun villagers all pounced on that statement.

"Wait, Chief? We thought you went squid hunting, but you were just taking a walk? Slacking off again?!"

"You *just* went sunbathing in the desert the other day! So irresponsible!"

"Oh, whatever! I came back before it got dark!" Alka argued, like a kid being scolded for playing in a vacant lot. The whole world was her playground...apparently?

Lloyd seemed to have heard similar conversations before. He was just putting more *shutou* sauce on, thoroughly enjoy the flavor.

"Mm, this really tastes like home! You just can't get flavors like this in the city. Maybe I just have blue-collar tastes."

"Yeah, no…"

This wasn't an entirely working-class dish.

But Merthophan just kept calmly explaining what was in the food. If you looked closely, his eyes were totally dead. Like he was long past rational thought. If every meal you ate involved legends and supernatural phenomena, you'd get that way. This was a necessary defense mechanism to retain a shred of sanity.

Once everyone was full…well, the Azami contingent all looked like they'd got a bad case of indigestion. That happened when you had a belly full of end game monsters and international issues.

"Right, clear away these fish bones!" the housekeeper said.

Eyes gleaming, Riho shot to her feet. "I'll help clean!"

"Oh, the beady-eyed girl! You're a guest today, so you just sit back and relax."

"No, no, after a feast like that, it's the least I can do!"

The housekeeper gave her a warm smile. "Then by all means!" They headed out back.

"……She's definitely collecting materials."

Everyone who knew Riho nodded. When Riho came back, beaming, her pockets were bulging.

"You don't miss a beat, huh?" Eug said, guzzling a beer. She flashed her canines at Riho approvingly.

The party was in full swing, and the villagers were six cups deep. One middle-aged woman sidled over to Lloyd, whispering in his ear.

"Lloyd, which of these is your girlfriend?"

This killer pass caught Lloyd entirely off guard.

"N-none of them! They're all from my school. No girlfriends!"

Their conversation instantly had the girls' undivided attention.

Grinning, the villagers began joining in.

"Oh? I thought you'd come back to introduce us! Grandpa Pyrid was all ready to be a great-grandpa!"

"Well, even if he doesn't have one now, Lloyd's the right age! He's at least interested in *someone*!"

The ceaseless attacks were tearing Lloyd apart. And the girls were starting to fidget, all leaning forward.

A new killer pass shot in from a totally different direction.

"Well, if I had to pick one, I'd go for Riho."

"Yeah, no complaints about her."

Suddenly thrust into the limelight, Riho spit tea everywhere.

"Huhaarrghhh?!" was all she managed, deeply flummoxed. She'd never expected anyone to push for her.

Meanwhile, the villagers began explaining their logic.

"Yeah, she jumps right in to help with everything! She's considerate!"

"She only just got here, and she was already helping Grandpa Pyrid with that fish! She respects her elders! Such a good girl."

Her passion for high-level materials had received a very favorable interpretation. Since none of this was intentional, Riho was turning bright red but also not arguing. There had to be a part of her deep down that was all for getting closer to Lloyd…if only she could be honest with herself.

The Azami girls and Alka were all glaring daggers. Chrome, Choline, and Merthophan all knew her real motives and were stifling laughs.

""""Tch…"""""

Selen, Phyllo, Marie, and Alka weren't laughing at all. Their tongues were cracking like whips. Maybe these four are a little *too* honest.

Early reporting was showing Riho with a commanding lead in the polls, ready to claim a majority of seats, but then a new candidate appeared.

"Hold on now!" Grandpa Pyrid stepped in. "I'm nominating Phyllo!"

This was the man who'd raised Lloyd and commanded a great deal of authority in Kunlun. And he'd just thrown his weight behind Phyllo as Lloyd's future wife.

"We sparred a bit earlier, but she's a good 'un. She'd adapt to life out here in the boonies real quick. She's a promising fighter and would do good work for us."

A faint smirk appeared on Phyllo's poker face. She wasn't a particularly "good" one.

"............I win," she whispered.

Grandpa Pyrid was Lloyd's father figure, so his backing her was like parents bowing and saying, "Please take care of our daughter." Oh, well, Lloyd was a boy, but…well, he could cook, so it *could* work. Phyllo's triumphant look suggested she was ready to head straight through the goal to a victory lap in the bedroom, but the other girls all restrained her.

Selen was usually the most active of Lloyd's suitors, but Riho and Phyllo had a ten-length lead in this horse race. She was biting her nails in frustration. And screeching.

Unable to bear it, Vritra tried to console her.

"Mistress, you haven't lost yet! Maintain composure…!"

If the balance of power didn't shift soon, he was in for a full night of griping. His desperation was clear.

Selen surprised him with a show of strength.

"Hmph!" she huffed. "I'm disappointed to hear his father figure pick someone else, true. But it's not like I've been standing silently by."

"Oh? You have a plan, then?"

"If you can't shoot the general, shoot his horse. Heh-heh…this is why I've been letting the village kids play with my belt! Raising my approval ratings that way!"

"So that's why you forced me to entertain them despite my protests…"

Guess that went down during the chapter break.

From Vritra's perspective, this had involved a lot of innocent voices yelping, "A talking belt!" and patting him all over with dirty hands. He'd endured. After all, if he disobeyed one of Selen's orders, there was no telling *what* she'd do to him later.

"Grown-up opinions hold no power before the demands of children! If they start saying, 'Mommy, I want Lloyd to marry Selen!' everyone will have to answer, 'Okay, fine, just this once.' Then the kids'll be all, 'I love you, Mommy!' and it'll be perfect!"

She'd found a whole new breed of delusion!

At any rate, Selen's strategy was to shoo herself into the wife race by making herself popular with the kids. If you'll excuse the blunt metaphor, it's like Christmas season toy ads forcing loaded parents to drop a fat wad of cash on their kids.

"I find it hard to approve of manipulating children," Vritra said, cringing visibly. "Is there no other way?"

Selen's face twisted into a demon mask. "I'm allowing you to stay rent free in my belt? And you dare talk back?!"

"Er, this belt was originally part of my back, but...forgive my previous rudeness!"

Vritra bowed his buckle repeatedly. Like a worker dealing with a temperamental boss.

"That's even worse! Because you let Alka rip your skin off so easily, the resulting curse ruined my entire childhood! You owe me big-time!"

"I cannot apologize for that myself! I had no idea my rage would manifest in—"

"But because of that, I met Sir Lloyd, so we're good. But if I can't hook up with him, I'm nothing but a clown!"

Selen had definitely been a clown so far, but she leaped to her feet, yelled, "Follow me!" and attempted to lead an army of children forward like the Pied Piper.

"Come, children! Now is your moment to back me!"

But the children she'd placed her faith in...

"Is that a metal arm?!"

"Oh, hey, careful, don't touch that."

"Whoa! How does it move?"

"Uh, with magic?"

The children in question had decided Riho's mithril arm was way cooler than Selen's belt. A creepy wriggling strap never stood a chance against the feature-rich metal gleam of Riho's appendage. Few would blame them.

"Childreeeeeeeeen?!" Selen fell to her knees. She had sorely over-estimated their attention span.

"An artificial limb at your age... You must have a tragic past."

"How you must have suffered."

"And despite that, she grew up straight and true!"

Not really.

Adding insult to injury, the parents were all making sweeping assumptions and tearing up over them. Riho's popularity was sky-rocketing to Ghibli levels of cross-generational appeal.

"Arghhh...a belt that can move and talk makes an impression, but carries no style points! Do you have any good ideas, Vritra? I need a plan to break free of this bind!"

"Mistress Selen! I have an idea!"

"Oh? Let's hear it."

"If you follow the talking belt to its logical extreme and transform into a magical girl, the children will love it!"

"Pfft, nobody cares about magical girls anymore!"

Er, they're quite popular... Like, really in vogue... Did she not watch TV on Sunday mornings? Selen seemed to be as oblivious to current fads as she was ethics.

Cut down, Vritra hung the buckle he was using in place of a head.

"Hngg...I see... When 'my children' were little, they watched such shows with their parents, but..."

This turn of phrase struck Selen as rather odd.

"Oh? The guardian beast of Kunlun has children? More big snakes?"

"My children are...mm. That is odd."

Eug leaned in, as if cutting that conversation off.

"You talking transformations?" she asked enthusiastically. "That sounds fun! Let me join in."

No mad scientist could resist *that* word.

"E-Eug! No, I…"

"Vri, don't you worry about a thing! You want me to turn you into something other than a snake? I can make you tall and handsome! You want a nose job? A cleft chin?"

Now it was just plastic surgery.

"H-handsome?" This word seemed to tempt him momentarily.

"Well? I sure don't mind."

"Th-then by all means!"

Eug grinned, pulled out a pencil, and started doodling a final design.

When she had the sketch, she held it up so Vritra could see—only looking *mildly* evil.

"Right, here's the final version! A giant one-eyed frog! Your new form!"

"Good heavens, no! It fits none of the designated parameters! What happened to tall and handsome?!"

"Well, I gotta lot of frog meat lying around, so…and you know, frog faces are kinda handsome, if you look at them the right way! And it's tall for a frog! That's why I made it giant! The one-eye…well, that's just a bonus!"

"You don't subtract an eye as a bonus! Going from a snake to a frog is clearly a downgrade! A predator becoming prey has entirely flubbed his career transition!"

"Eug," Selen said. "Our goal here is to earn the love of children, so I don't think a frog would really do it."

"Then…a cat or a dog?"

"We seem to have lost sight of the real goal here! This is about restoring me!"

The discussion had become more like a toy company planning a new product line.

Poor Vritra. But he wasn't the worst person off here.

"Augh…"

That would be Marie. Not one person had her back in the wife-off, and she was on the verge of tears.

All around her, arguments about Lloyd's wife were reaching a fever pitch. Since no one else was nominating her, she considered throwing her hat in the ring…but that would amount to asking him out.

Before she could take that bold step, she got hit again—mercilessly.

"You're his landlord, right? Who would you pick?"

"Huh? Landlord?!"

The man addressing her was definitely pretty drunk. Marie had never considered herself a landlord before, but the man was way too drunk to notice her confusion.

"You're running the place where Lloyd stays, right? You see Lloyd with these girls all the time. Who do you think is best for him?"

"………Damn you, kid grandma…" Marie glared at Alka. "That was how you introduced me?!"

"Bwa-ha-ha-ha-ha!" Alka doubled over, laughing and clutching her stomach. She'd successfully blocked Marie's entry in the race! How cruel!

The landlord. If this were a dating sim, she'd be a locked route at best—if not a supporting character. Marie's tears were starting to flow.

"Huh? Was the chief wrong about that? Why are you crying?"

"Oh, don't worry about her! The waterworks come on the moment she gets a few drinks in her! Typical landlord, huh?"

Meanwhile, the wife race was really picking up.

"What do you say? He may be young, but he is a soldier! Will you take Lloyd as your bride?"

"Augh, don't say that! I'm a guy! I can't be a bride!"

The villagers' enthusiasm left Lloyd fuming, but everyone just laughed.

Left in the dust, Riho was just sitting very still, beet red, staring at her hands.

Lloyd desperately tried to change the subject.

"I've got a long way ahead of me. The only reason I'm a soldier at all is because of Allan."

"Oh? You owe him, then?"

"Yeah. I failed the exam once, but he saw potential in me and rec-ommended they take me on. And all he wants me to do in return is to teach him how to cook."

Lloyd had never realized it, but he'd saved Allan from a monster attack, and in exchange, Allan had traded an offer of promotion to get Lloyd enlisted. When Allan talked about being Lloyd's disciple, he meant combat—not cooking.

But all the listening villagers were very pleased with what Allan had done.

"I see! This boy sounds like a saint! We'll have to thank him properly later. If he were a girl, we'd add him to the list of brides…then again, if Lloyd just agrees to *be* the bride…"

"Ha-ha-ha-ha-ha-ha…!" Everyone laughed again.

The conversation was going off the rails again.

"Doesn't matter who Lloyd marries," slurred a guy who'd been like a brother to Lloyd. "Even a man would be better than the chief!"

"True enough!"

"Ha-ha-ha-ha-ha-ha…!" Another round of laughter.

Reduced to a punch line, Alka was sobbing loudly.

Eug gave her a reassuring pat on the back.

"I totally agree! That boy's way too good for you."

"Don't act like you're comforting me only to kick me when I'm down! You always do that!"

"Now, now, I *am* comforting you. And we should have a drink later! We haven't seen each other in a while. We got lots of catching up to do."

"Mm. All right, everyone! Time we wrap stuff up!"

The villagers started getting ready to leave.

The guests headed off to their rooms.

Alka was looking up at the stars above. A beautiful night view.

They were in the chief's room, and the two of them were sitting on chairs of woven bamboo.

Eug was sitting across from Alka. She pulled out a bottle of amber liquid—whiskey.

"Drink with me, Alka. You like it straight, right?"

Alka nodded.

"This liver goes through poison like there's no tomorrow—I can't even get tipsy from mixed drinks. An unpleasant reminder of my immortality."

"I remember when a single drink would knock you out… Here."

Alka held the glass of amber liquid up to her nose, savoring the odor.

"That's a rich scent—what's the maker?"

"Mm? I dunno, something-or-other-whiskey. Pretty sure it's a thousand years old."

"A thousand?"

"Theoretically. It's aged artificially with an ultrasonic device, but if I'm being totally honest, I couldn't tell the difference between five hundred years and a thousand."

Alka raised an eyebrow and then took a sip.

She took another long sniff. "You're always inventing these crazy gizmos. And this morning, you suddenly started babbling about viruses… Nobody knew what you were talking about."

Eug took a sip of her own whiskey, not looking the least bit sorry.

"If they don't understand a word of it, what's the harm?"

"You know better. Never know who might be watching… C'mon, another."

Alka's cheeks were slightly flushed, but she held out her glass.

Glug glug glug…the room filled with the sound of her glass filling.

She knocked the entire glass back and let out a boozy sigh.

"I think I know what you wanna talk about," Alka said.

"You ran into him, right? I wanna know what you made of him."

Eug leaned forward over the table, with an expression of great interest.

Alka looked increasingly gloomy.

"You mean Sou, right? He's failed in his efforts, but he's still scheming. Maybe he thinks if he turns evil, he can finally disappear for good. One of our villagers has himself mixed up in it. Seems like they're behind the unusually high numbers of demon lords or things split off from them."

"Nobody would ever believe he was the legendary hero, Sou."

"When he rounded up all the demon lords and flung them in the final prison, his role should have ended. But instead of fading out, he was restored to the world. Never the most stable man, he desperately wants to stop being the hero."

She looked up at the sky, speaking softly, as though to herself.

"But freeing all the captured demon lords will never do. Not with the world finally stable."

It was rare to see Alka look this serious. Eug folded her arms, every bit as solemn.

"Alka," she proposed. "Think it's time to move to the next stage?"

"The next stage?"

Eug popped the lollipop out of her mouth, pointing it at Alka.

"Did you forget? Develop the world, return things to the level they used to be."

"You mean…how things were back then?"

"Yeah," Eug said, flashing a sly grin. "That witch…she's the princess of Azami, right? If we start an industrial revolution there, well, they've got the prosperity to handle it, even if we move fast. Remember how great it was? Cars and planes everywhere? You could order anything you wanted with the tip of your finger."

"But is there a need to develop the world right now?"

"Yeah. Magic research has progressed far enough. There are even people out there trying to decipher runes. That means we can expect real progress, mixing magic and science together in new ways. We'll see a whole new world, one we could never have in the old days. And if we keep the Last Dungeon under control, the demon lords aren't a threat—and we can get our lost comrades back the way they were."

But the more Eug's eyes sparkled, the gloomier Alka got.

"Wishful thinking. We can't act on that alone. Or it'll all happen again."

"This is our entire purpose! And if we don't act soon, the Last Dungeon will bust open, and some so-called demon lords'll make the world a living hell again. Like you said—it'll all happen again."

A silence fell.

For a long while, the only sounds were their chairs creaking and the ice in Eug's glass clinking.

Finally, Eug spoke again. "You heard him earlier, right? Vritra—Director Ishikura almost remembered."

"Haven't heard that name in a while," Alka said, gazing at her reflection in the glass.

Eug's chair creaked as she leaned back, looking up at the stars.

"Yeah, he remembered watching anime with his kids. I jumped in and averted the crisis, but…if he remembers more, no telling what he'll do in his confusion."

She turned her eyes back to Alka, leaning forward.

"If we force him back to normal here without his kids? He might well go after the Last Dungeon. Vritra's not the only one. Even the demon lords were once—"

Alka shot her a look, cutting her off. "They might replace us, remake this world to their liking, abusing runes…"

"Yeah. But if this world can create a magic-science hybrid that can control the Last Dungeon, and restore what lies in those depths…or add magic to science to make something even better…"

Alka stared into her glass again.

Realizing Alka couldn't bring herself to take the next step, Eug sighed, shaking her head.

"I can't do it on my own. I may be the king of dwarves, but they don't care about anything except their work. I need you working with me. We need to restore the forms our old comrades lost and get back true peace."

"I know…but can't it wait a while longer?"

They stared up at the stars together.

"I've waited too long already," Eug said softly. So softly, Alka never heard.

The words vanished into the stars above.

Under that same starry sky, in another room of that same house, Merthophan was on his hands and knees, his forehead plastered to the ground.

"I can't apologize enough!"

He was prostrated before Marie. Chrome and Choline were sitting behind her, sipping their drinks and wincing.

Marie was forced into this position a lot herself, so being on the receiving end was especially awkward.

"That's enough! Raise your head. I can't take this. It's like I'm seeing myself genuflect before the kid grandma..."

Like having a mirror held up to her own behavior. Marie had a much larger repertoire of kowtows, with variations that included choked sobs and lots of snot, and these provided observers (well, Alka) with no end of entertainment.

Merthophan's head jerked up. "Thank you for your kind words, Princess Maria! This is a daikon radish from my fields!"

He produced a giant white vegetable and held it out, tears of gratitude streaming down his face.

"Uh...this isn't the best timing..."

"Good point! I'll give it to you—with plenty of other veggies—on your way home!"

He wrapped the daikon up in a nice cloth and then topped off her glass. Anyone who knew his history would be horrified at this display of servility—the faces of his former colleagues proved as much.

But the mention of their departure put a question in Choline's mind. Cheeks somewhat flushed from the alcohol, she asked, "Are you ever coming back to Azami, Merthophan?"

"Not anytime soon," he said, looking grim. "I may have been under the thumb of a demon lord, but I still tried to overthrow the monarchy."

"Yeah…I figured."

She still looked disappointed.

His expression grew even grimmer.

"And if I leave Kunlun, my children—the crops I've worked so hard to grow—won't have anyone to look after them."

"R-right…," Chrome managed to say. Having crops called children sent a shudder down his spine.

"When I first got here, everything was so outlandish that my mind couldn't handle it. I was afraid to face the dawn. But thanks to my crops, I'm looking forward to each new day."

Incidentally, Kunlun produce could be harvested a month after planting them—way beyond what was achievable with selective breeding or genetic modification.

The need to gather all those crops every month was a lot of work, even with the power Kunlun villagers possessed…especially since Alka always disappeared at harvest time—like a part-timer who always puts in for paid time off when they know the shop is going to be jam-packed because of a promotional campaign.

"That demon lord… Can you tell us more about him? The kid gra— Chief Alka won't really get specific."

Marie had asked about demon lords any number of times, but Alka always just dismissed them as a "pain in her backside."

"I know the memories must be painful, but any information you have on demon lords would really help."

Merthophan groaned thoughtfully. "I had a grudge against the Jiou Empire," he said. The words did not come easily to him. "I believed they were responsible for the destruction of my home. And my anger about them grew and grew…and then a merchant appeared before me."

"A merchant?"

"Yes—he spoke the words I wished to hear and handed me a jewel, like a sinister egg, instructing me to give that to the Azami king…"

"That's strange," Chrome said, breaking in. "I can't imagine you accepting something like that from a total stranger, much less handing it to the king."

Merthophan was a real stickler for the rules. He would never accept the kind of bribes or the sort of underhanded dealings that often went down between merchants and military leaders.

"Yeah, in hindsight, I have no idea what I was thinking. But at the time, I never doubted my actions. I was driven to act, without hesitation—some sort of mind control, if you'll forgive me making excuses."

He bowed his head again, to Marie's chagrin.

"That's about when ya asked me to start researching runes, right?" Choline popped in. "I thought it was strange, considering you never knew much about magic."

"It seems likely… My memories are rather fuzzy."

Merthophan frowned, lost in thought.

Marie went back to the point. "Can you describe this merchant at all?"

"Sorry, I'm not even sure he *was* a merchant. I know he was a man, maybe thirty? Or sixty…oh! Right."

"You remembered something else?"

"The man asked what he looked like to me. And I said he was proba-bly some sort of merchant…"

When he added this, Chrome and Choline both sat up.

"Choline, do you think…?"

"Chrome, could this merchant be behind…?"

"Behind what?" Marie asked.

Chrome filled her in on the reports of people going missing, and the strange man who'd been witnessed asking what people saw him as.

The more she heard, the grimmer Marie's expression grew.

"So Abaddon may have been the demon lord that possessed my father, but there was someone else behind his actions?"

And they were potentially trying for a repeat. A chilling thought.

Silence settled over the room. It was broken by a knock at the door—and Lloyd, bearing tea.

"Hey, everyone. I figured you could use some tea!"

His cheery voice immediately lifted everyone's spirits.

"Thanks, Lloyd!"

He handed each of them a cup. Merthophan got a glass of grape juice.

"What's this?" Merthophan asked.

"Oh," Lloyd said with a genuine smile. "I know you have a troubled history with alcohol, so I figured you were abstaining. And I thought you might want a little something extra to keep them company."

It was like he was offering the designated driver a nonalcoholic beer.

"Er, right…," Merthophan managed.

He was a driven patriot, yet Lloyd seemed to view him as nothing but an ex-drunk turned teetotaler.

"I'm sure you don't remember any of it, but you made a mess of yourself during the festival. Dressing up as some weird insect thing, staggering around drunk…"

Now he was a tipsy cosplayer, apparently. Merthophan fought back his tears.

"I can't apologize enough for that," he croaked.

"I heard there were monsters around, too! But Marie took care of those… I'm glad everything ended safely. I hope you can get back to work soon! I'm sure you have a lot to teach me."

Lloyd bowed his head and left the room.

The silence in his wake was even longer.

"Um, does…he not know how strong he is?"

"He's the weakest person in Kunlun, apparently."

There was a brief pause.

"Feels silly to worry about anything now…"

With Lloyd and Kunlun around, no demon lord could possibly pose a threat. The grim looks were a thing of the past.

Now, in yet another room—the three cadet girls had their futons lined up in a row.

Picture the standard school trip, girls with heads pressed together, whispering about which boys they're gonna ask out—this wasn't that. After all, it was already obvious who they liked.

"…What?" Riho said, eyes half-lidded, covers pulled up. With her hair down like this, she seemed significantly less tomboyish—even hints of cute.

Selen and Phyllo were both staring at her—and she wasn't about to back down from *that* challenge.

"You're cheating."

"…Cheating," Phyllo echoed.

"Oh, shut up! This isn't my fault! What's with the staring contest anyway?" Riho threw her covers back, leaping into a fighting stance.

"We're monitoring you so you don't sneak into his bedroom in the cover of night."

"I ain't that dumb!"

"…I would totally do it," Phyllo declared. A problem in itself.

"Why do they all love you?! They even gave you new clothes!" Selen protested.

"Nah, they don't…"

"…They do. And I heard those clothes are really nice."

"Huh? They are?"

Riho blinked at her. Phyllo explained further.

"…They're made from superior silk gathered from earth spiders."

Earth spiders. Another high-level monster. The face of a demon, the body of a tiger, and the legs of a spider. A hideous beast, indeed. The venom in their fangs would leave you running a high fever for three days and nights.

©Nao Watanuki

If one bit a Kunlun villager, it would be no more effective than a mosquito sting…since they all had high poison resistance.

"See! Those clothes prove they love you! Argh, I'm so jealous!"

Before Selen had even finished ranting, Riho was up and inspecting her clothing.

"Whoa, really? Earth spider silk is crazy valuable!"

She ran her fingers down the sleeves, checking the quality. She even flipped her skirt up to inspect her underwear. Shameless!

"Ah, Riho! Don't do that!"

Even Selen balked.

Wholly ignoring the other girl, Riho completed her detailed exploration of her underwear and nodded happily.

"Come to think of it, these are super comfortable! I guess I was right not to bring any underwear!"

Something no girl should *ever* say…but immediately afterward, Riho started stripping.

"I can't wear these!"

Even Phyllo looked genuinely shocked at this sudden striptease.

"…Um, didn't you already take a bath?"

"Don't be silly! I'm getting out of these clothes before I get them dirty or wrinkled! I gotta sell them!"

"Do you have a replacement?"

"I can sleep naked! Is there a hanger in here? Oh, found one! Careful with 'em, careful…heh-heh…"

Lovingly hanging her clothes and underwear on the hangers, she made sure there were no wrinkles. In later days, Phyllo would claim the sight of her wickedly grinning as she smoothed out the fabric of her panties was almost awe-inspiring.

At this exact moment…

There was a knock on the door and a gentle voice.

"Pardon me."

"Y-yes?" Riho yelped a bit. She was still naked, after all. Apparently, this was the *wrong* choice of words, because Lloyd took that as permission to enter.

"I brought you some tea, so—"

When the door opened, he found himself face-to-face with all of Riho.

""!!!!!!!!!""

Silent screams all around.

"...............Hah!" Phyllo's instinctive reaction was to kick Lloyd as hard as she could.

Ka-thunk!

It happened so fast, Lloyd didn't have time to dodge. He shot out the window behind him into the starry sky above.

"...I never expected to kick my master away."

There was a tinge of regret on Phyllo's face.

Meanwhile, Selen's expression had gone eerily blank. She pointed at Riho.

"Get dressed."

"Yes, sorry," Riho whispered. She obediently donned her clothes.

"As punishment, we're going to tie you up now."

"Yes, sorry."

Riho allowed herself to be bound hand and foot.

She was too mortified to sleep a wink anyway.

"Definitely bringing underwear next time...definitely..."

A change of underwear is a must-have for any traveler.

Kunlun was bathed in the dawn's gentle sunlight.

Greenery was showered in the morning mist. Well, the plants *looked* like weeds, but they were actually medicinal herbs used to make a panacea. Eaten straight, they could numb your whole mouth and gradually paralyze your entire body, so you really needed to know how to handle them.

A flock of small birds flew past. Well, killing birds. Known as the piranhas of the skies, each of them alone was no real threat, but harm one, and the entire flock would come after you, pecking until not even your bones remained.

It was a peaceful morning…where one false step would send you straight to hell.

"Whoaaaaa, what happened to you last night?"

Her white coat gleaming in the morning sunlight, Eug rolled her lollipop around her mouth, looking from Lloyd to Riho.

"N-nothing."

"N-nothing at all."

This aroused Alka's suspicion. "No! Something untoward happened without me noticing?!"

"Never fear," Selen snapped. "It certainly wasn't what *you're* imagining. We tied her up to prevent *that*."

The belt at Selen's waist—Vritra—bowed apologetically.

"I cannot refuse an order from her. I hope it wasn't too trying."

"Nah, it was…pretty much what I deserved. Argh."

Just the memory of it made Riho turn beet red.

"Well, then fine… So what do you all want?"

"Do I have to remind you again, Alka?! The restoration of my flesh and blood! If I remain in this unstable condition, I might well vanish forever! And then you'll no longer be able to control your power! You might even break the seal on the Last Dungeon!"

"Oh, I remember now."

"You have always been like this," Vritra said, exasperated. "You never listen to anyone else! Even on our quest to save the world, you let critical information go in one ear and out the other! You even forgot information you personally gathered! No matter how many times I told you to stamp those documents, you never remembered! A poor example to the staff at large!"

Lloyd and Marie were confused by the sudden reference to stamping documents.

Eug hastily jumped in. "Well, here we are! Our destination!"

The top of a building peered above the surface of the ground, almost like a dungeon.

Crumbling white walls, revealing the iron within. The walls themselves weren't natural stone, but some sort of gray brick.

None of them had ever seen anything built like this or the materials involved. They gazed at it in wonder.

"*Is* this a dungeon?" Selen asked.

"Yup, the final prison—the Last Dungeon."

"Ugh, coming here always reminds me of my own weaknesses…," Eug said gloomily.

"Last…?" Riho said. "That sounds like there's crazy treasure in there! Are we going in?"

Alka grabbed her before she could take another step.

"This is where the demon lords slumber."

"The…demon lords?" Riho yelped, thoroughly rattled.

She'd been traumatized enough by one the day before.

And Riho wasn't the only one who shuddered at the thought. They exchanged nervous glances.

Oblivious to this, Eug offered additional details. "Dungeons are essentially prisons. The Last Dungeon is the most remote of those. They aren't monster-and-treasure-filled lairs like you're imagining."

The look in Eug's eyes made it clear she had a history with this place.

"We subdue or negotiate with demon lords whenever they threaten us and seal them away in here. Not all of them, and sometimes they escape…like Abaddon or the Erlking. The dungeons you all know are essentially camouflage meant to hide the Last Dungeon. We dwarves built them the world over, in this dungeon's image."

"Th-the dwarves made the dungeons?!" Riho yelped.

"And they got a bit carried away with it. Making dungeons became a way for dwarves to show off their skills. They got obsessed with designing traps and secret passages, and filled treasure chests with their crafts, daring people to find them. Artisan spirit at its worst."

A shocking truth would definitely make any academic spray snot and assuredly surprised everyone here.

"Even if I told everyone, they'd never believe me," Choline said.

"Certainly not," Chrome replied, shaking his head. "You'd have to start by proving dwarves really exist. That alone would be considered an earth-shattering discovery."

The question of why dungeons had traps and treasure in them had long been a subject of debate, but the existence of dwarves and Kunlun would be even more sensational news.

Meanwhile, Alka was staring grimly at the Last Dungeon.

"The Last Dungeon," she said. "It is the duty of Kunlun villagers to subdue the demon lords that emerge from these depths."

"I-it is?!" Lloyd yelped. "I've never seen one, but…demon lords sound real scary! I can't even defeat a monster on my own, so I'd never stand a chance!"

He hadn't realized it, but he had actually beaten a treant demon lord on his own. Everyone just let his self-esteem issues slide these days.

Eug pointed at Vritra. He flinched.

"Vritra is Kunlun's—and Alka's—guardian beast. Because she can deflect all damage to Vritra, Alka can control and abuse the power that emerges from the Last Dungeon without it destroying her."

"Her power comes from the dungeon?" Riho asked. "What exactly *is* this place?"

"Curious?" Eug asked, grinning. "Something down there makes manifest that which people the world over, in the collective unconscious, assume to be true. Think of it as a world-scale rune. We're using the ancient script and fairy tales to make the world perceive Alka as the priestess of salvation and Vritra as the guardian beast."

Eug was rattling off a bunch of jargon, her lab coat swirling—but no one listening understood a word of it.

Realizing this could go on awhile, Marie cut in.

"So Master forgot how important this was, cut part of Vritra's skin off, and made an apron out of it, thus causing this entire situation? What is *wrong* with you?"

"Eug forgot about it, too!" Alka protested. "It was her idea to cut part of his skin off!"

"Never mind that!" Eug said.

Everyone glared at her, but she ignored it.

"If Vritra vanishes and Alka's power can't be controlled—it's already pretty unstable—then all someone needs is the key, and all the demon lords will come pouring out. Worst-case scenario."

"The key?"

Eug scratched her head, looking at Alka. "What, did you not tell them? The Holy Sword. The one Azami tried to turn into a prize at the sorcery tournament."

"Er...isn't that super dangerous, then?" Marie said, looking guilty. She was the one who'd tricked Lloyd into pulling it in the first place.

"I dunno why it was pulled or who pulled it, but I think they also pulled all the hair out of that poor mayor's head."

Pretty sure he'd been bald to begin with. Had been since his early twenties, an extreme early onset of male pattern baldness... Well, that doesn't have so much as a single hair of relevance to this story, so let's just move on.

"What-a-mystery!" Marie said in a monotone, with a frozen grin.

Eug genuinely didn't seem to care who'd pulled it out. She had a different question for Alka.

"Well, like that mayor's hair, once it's been yanked, it ain't coming back—so where is it now?"

"I think it's in safekeeping at the Azami castle."

"Okay. Take good care of it." Eug turned to Selen. "Bring the cursed belt... No, bring Vritra over here."

"Uh, okay..."

Selen undid the belt's buckles.

"Good-bye, Vritra," she said tenderly. "Life with you was not at all bad."

"Yes, yes, I regret that we must part, mistress! Beyond all measure!" Vritra insisted. Then, under his breath, he whispered, "…Freedom."

The truth comes out. Oblivious to this, Selen was actually on the verge of tears. If Vritra hadn't been a belt, he would have likely been crying, too. Tears of joy, that is.

Eug took Vritra from her and laid the belt out on some machinery she had set up.

Nothing about this seemed remotely occult—it was more like a production line, gears everywhere. When Eug touched it, steam started pumping out.

"Thanks…let's begin the ritual to restore Vritra!"

This looked less like a ceremony than weapon forging. The gears started churning, clanking loudly.

"Thank you, Eug," Alka expressed.

Eug removed some ingredients from a pouch. "We need meat… Snake was too much of a pain, so it's just beef."

She slapped the hunk of beef on the machines.

"And some purifying salt!"

Eug took a pinch of coarse salt and sprinkled it over the meat. This looked indistinguishable from basic meal prep, but no one dared point that out.

"Next, wrap the beef in the belt. Carefully, so it doesn't lose shape or fall apart."

The way she tied it looked awfully like tying a roast. Still, no one dared say anything.

"And then we add my special culture fluid and simmer over low heat…"

"Hold on a moment! Are you sure you aren't trying to cook me?" Vritra said.

The amber fluid she was basting with sure looked a lot like soy sauce.

"Ya got me! Sorry, sorry."

She didn't look the least bit apologetic. Vritra protested, but since he was trapped in the belt, he was no more able to resist than a captured eel.

"You have always been—"

"Now here's the real deal, Vri. Behave."

With that, she blew something on him.

"Hngg...unh..."

The belt writhed like it had been struck by lightning.

Eug rewrapped the meat, then pressed it against something palm-sized and round, like an eggshell. It clearly wasn't large enough for Vritra and the meat to fit inside, but...for some reason, they were inserted easily.

Eug produced some sort of machine—it looked like a vise—and began applying pressure. Steam billowed out of the device, obscuring the view.

"Blegh, what the heck is this?" Alka said. "Eug and her crazy gizmos..."

The dwarf emerged from the vapor cloud, wearing goggles. She grinned wide enough to flash her canines, tossing the egg from hand to hand.

"All done! Oh, Alka, c'mere a minute," she urged, waving Alka over.

The egg-shaped shell in her hands was semi-translucent. There was a faint glow within.

"Mm? What? Need my help?"

"Yep, gimme your forehead."

Grinning wickedly, Eug proceeded to flick Alka repeatedly.

"Ow! Owwwwww! Why does it hurt?! That actually hurts!"

Alka clutched her forehead, writhing in agony—like a rookie comedian trying to make a name for herself in physical comedy.

Eug bared her fangs again, laughing. "Ah-ha-ha-ha-ha! Didn't expect you to be such a baby about it! But cool. I *am* a genius."

"Not cool! Ohh..."

"Ch-Chief?"

Alka had gone limp, and Lloyd scrambled to catch her.

She would normally seize that chance to cop a few feels, but today she didn't even try.

"Ugh, what is this? The perfect chance to grope Lloyd, but my body just feels all wrong..."

That clinched it. Everyone was now actively worried about her. Something was clearly wrong.

"The kid grandma..."

"The personification of sexual harassment..."

"My rival stalk—I mean, romantic!"

".......That pervert?"

"Baseless accusations!" Alka barked.

Really?

Eug looked around at each of them, smirking.

"She's definitely weakened. I *thought* doing the ritual in proximity to the Last Dungeon would up the odds of success! The device that manifests the collective unconscious is effective. Oh, I'm positively shaking!"

"She's...weakened?"

"Yup. This proves Alka's connection to the Last Dungeon is completely severed. You wanna get some payback? Bury her in a ditch? Now's your chance! She can't fly or drop meteorites on you."

"Payback? Tempting...," Marie whispered, rubbing her hands together.

"You fool of a student!" Alka snarled. "You're thinking, 'Woohoo,' aren't you?"

"Hardly," Marie insisted. "It was more of a 'Hell yeah!' Oh, whoops..."

She'd gotten a bit carried away and let the truth slip out.

"That's worse, nincompoop! You might get away with it in the moment, but there'll be hell to pay later!"

"Uh, from time immemorial, ancient witches have had a habit of chanting 'Hell? Yeah...' when they feel pity."

"Mess with me, and you'll know true pain!"

"...........Whoops."

Marie had experienced enough of Alka's punishments. She was already quivering like a frightened puppy.

Watching this, Eug did a few stretches.

"Whew, now then. We're all done here—better head back. You've got an exhibition match coming up, right? Kind of a big deal for Azami, I hear."

"Hngg, right…we've got to prep for that."

"Looking forward to it myself!" Eug said. "Tomorrow, right? I figured I'd drop in. Got nothing else to do until Vri revives. You don't mind, do you, Alka?"

She snapped her sucker against her teeth and gave Alka a look like an eager child.

"Since when do you care about things like that?" Alka asked, looking exhausted. "But well…you did help with the restoration, so I owe you this one."

Alka glanced at Choline and Chrome.

Chrome nodded. "Yes, you've been a big help—we'd be happy to return the favor."

"We threw the match together on short notice, so we got plenty of good seats left. We can hook ya up."

"Ta," Eug said, then turned back to Alka. "Oh, right, Alka—hate to bug you when you're tired, but can we have a word?"

"A word?"

Eug was as energetic and cheerful as Alka was weak and worn out.

"Yup, yup! A few things to watch out for in your condition, when to expect the restoration to complete—just more of what was talked about yesterday. Don't wanna do that with everyone listening, do we?"

"Hmm…right. Okay, everyone, Eug and I need to chat. You go on ahead."

Everyone nodded and headed back to the village to pack up their things.

*   *   *

A rocky area a short distance from the Last Dungeon—the horned rabbits had hollowed out these rocks, leaving a network of tunnels, like an ant nest. Ordinary horned rabbits would never be capable of this, but Kunlun horned rabbits were way bigger. Their burrows were large enough for people to walk around in—a natural labyrinth where one false step spelled doom.

Alka and Eug were strolling through these tunnels together.

"Why come here to talk? Let's get this over with so I can take advantage of my weakened condition and make Lloyd spoil me...heh-heh-heh."

This last chuckle was totally in dirty old man territory.

"Do you remember?" Eug asked quietly. "We used to walk the halls of the lab like this, side by side, debating. Hard work, but rewarding."

"I remember. Hardly a healthy way to live. I never realized how good the sun feels."

Eug sighed. There was a trace of sadness behind it.

"You really did get addicted to the *isekai* slow life."

"Mm? What's that supposed to mean?"

"We talked about it yesterday. Are you still against developing this world to the baseline standards we used to have?"

Alka scratched her head, making a face.

"This again? I thought I rejected the idea already. What do I need to watch out for in this condition? I don't care about this dumb exhibition match, but I do wanna flirt with Lloyd."

"Phooey."

"What are you looking upset about? Y-you're not after Lloyd, too, are you?!"

Eug scowled at Alka. This was clearly way off-base.

"Obviously not," she snapped. "But clearly, we no longer think alike."

An instant later, Eug gave Alka's back a shove—with her foot.

Before Alka had time to react, she found herself in the air—falling.

"Uh...augh?! What the heeeeeell?!"

Roll, roll...sliiiiiide.

It took her a while after hitting the ground to realize she'd been dropped into a pit.

She'd spent so long with superhuman power that she'd forgotten how much bruises and scrapes hurt. Her face crumpled in agony.

"Ah, sorry, sorry—that was a bit too high for you in this condition, huh?"

Eug was peering over the edge. Alka put a hand on her aching neck, glaring up at her.

"Eug! What was that for? This isn't funny!"

"Not supposed to be. What I'm about to do is deadly serious."

"Huh?"

"I'm gonna open the Last Dungeon and release the demon lords into the world! Get it?"

Eug spoke without a trace of guilt, like she was confessing to a minor prank. Alka was left gaping up at her, unable to process this.

"If I can seal your power for a day or two, I can easily open the Last Dungeon. I know where the Holy Sword is, after all."

"No, wait! Don't!"

There was a rumble as Eug began dragging the stone door closed.

Alka frantically tried to scramble up the slope but ran out of energy before she was even halfway up.

"You'll never manage it with the power of a nine-year-old. You'll just hurt your little fingers!"

"Why are you doing this? This is way too sinister to count as payback!"

"This isn't payback—it's a declaration of war. I've made up my mind to force this world to develop itself until it can control the Last Dungeon...or the device within. If we apply magic and runes to science and our old standard of life—we can avoid a repeat of history."

"Eug! What are you talking about? How does that have anything to do with the demon lords?!"

"Plenty," Eug said, grinning. She talked just like she always did—or like a grown-up trying to talk sense into a child. "If we want humans to absorb new technology like a sponge, we need the threat the demon lords provide. Drowning men will grab any straw that comes their way. And I'm gonna send them a nuclear submarine. If their lives are in danger, it doesn't matter if the technology is completely unfamiliar; they'll use and research the hell out of it. Alka, you know full well how much war drove progress."

"Was Vritra's restoration a lie? A fib you used to seal my power?"

Eug pulled the egg she'd put Vritra in out of her pocket, rolling it around her palm.

"Exactly! The knowledge I gained from sealing away demon lords the world over sure came in handy. I can make use of him whenever I need another card up my sleeve! Reminds you of those old monster-hunting games, right?"

Alka was looking quite pale now.

"You mean...so this is why so many demon lords were showing up? Go to hell!"

"Your true colors are showing through, Alka. I thought you were the priestess of salvation."

Alka's eyes radiated pure hatred.

"Don't look at me like that," Eug said. "I'm acting out of the deepest respect for you, Alka."

"Eug..."

"But power or no power, if you get the Kunlun villagers to act, that'll be a thorn in my side. I'll need you to stay here for the time being. Don't worry! My plan is flawless."

"How can I not worry?! I can't sleep in the dark! At least drop a night-light down here!"

"Are you not ashamed to admit that?"

"Not in the least!"

Some people just couldn't sleep without a light on or on a different pillow...

Alka saw no shame in this at all. Eug looked down at her, an array of emotions running through her.

"Yeah, for all your talent, you never did have a sense of shame. Always slacking off. I couldn't believe it when I found you napping on a park bench near the lab, surrounded by salesmen."

"That's got nothing to do with this! C'mon! We're not some old bickering couple bringing up slights from our youth!"

Eug was clearly reminiscing, seeing someone else entirely when she looked at Alka.

"I was so weak then," she muttered, almost to herself. "I would never have dared argue with anyone who outranked me. If only I'd acted and made that plan fail...I can't forgive myself for being so powerless. The faster I can reject my past, the better."

She started closing the door once more.

"Eug, do you really think this will make the world as it was? Do you really think you can control that power enough to turn our friends back to what they were?"

Eug was starting to get fed up. She poked her head through the small remaining gap.

"Like I said, my plan is flawless," she snapped. "And I've found some reliable pawns. Wanna hint? 'Heroes.'"

"Heroes... You mean Sou and Shouma?"

Those two were working with Eug? Alka was unable to conceal her shock.

"They're both fixated on Lloyd. Once the world plunges into chaos, they'll make him... Whoops, that part is best left secret."

"Ah...I get it. One can't wait to die; the other just loves Lloyd to death. That explains why the two of them are working together. Such a stupid idea..."

Eug stuck her tongue out. She'd said too much.

"Welp, Alka, failure is the mother of success. We've got nigh eternal lives, so the best thing we can do is some trial and error."

"It's not like I don't get your point, but…"

Alka trailed off. Eug seemed to see right through her, going straight for the heart of the matter.

"You're just scared to lose them, huh? The Kunlun villagers, the people you've met. You got comfortable living in this fantasy world. And Lloyd—he looks exactly like the one you lost."

"……Don't you dare."

"I'm not stupid. I have a pretty good idea why you were studying the Last Dungeon, researching that system. And I know full well if it goes out of control again, it's bye-bye to the world as we know it."

Eug's tone grew cheery again.

"So don't worry! I'll be fiiine. And if it all goes well, you won't have to settle for Lloyd! We can make the real one!"

The hole was dark and chilly, but the words echoing through it were chillier still.

The door slid firmly closed.

"Eug! Eug! You fool! Don't you remember how that confidence betrayed you before?!"

An incline like this would have been no problem before. She could have shattered that stone door like a cookie. Frustration and rage had Alka's head spinning.

"You fool…Lloyd is Lloyd. The idea we could just…create people is what caused the accident in the first place… I don't want that. I don't want to lose any of them…"

There was a sob in her voice, but the only answer was the echoes rebounding from the depths of the chilly pit.

A while later…the guests from Azami were at Alka's house, packing up.

"Well," Choline said. "This place did nothing but shock us, but now that I'm leaving…I'll kinda miss it. Wouldn't have minded staying a bit longer."

"You mean that?" Chrome asked, frowning.

"Well…the food was good, I guess. But having every meal made from ingredients that could pay for a house with a nice garden back home does sure shrivel the stomach. Once a year is about all I can handle."

"Once a year, huh? I think it's a nice village, with good people in it, but kids, grown-ups, and ladies alike are all such powerhouses. Being here really frays the nerves."

Choline seemed to have rationalized it the way people do their annual vacation in Hawaii. On the other hand, Chrome felt like the one good citizen hanging out in a bar filled with hit men. He knew they weren't actually trying to kill him but couldn't shake the feeling that one wrong move would be his doom. The kind of party where no amount of booze can get him drunk.

"It was full of surprises, but a lovely place! I just have to find a way to get a bit more used to it somehow, and then I can live happily in matrimonial bliss!"

Nothing seemed to dissuade Selen for long. It was almost worthy of respect. On its own.

"…It was very educational. If I can marry Master, I *know* I can reach greater heights still."

Phyllo was also impossible to dissuade. She seemed just as focused on making herself stronger as she was on Lloyd.

"…………After what he saw………how can I ever face him again…?"

The problem was Riho. Her greedy core was still there, but she'd fallen hard for Lloyd pretty fast. She'd occasionally let glimpses of a girl with a crush emerge from that hardened shell…but now mortification had overwhelmed all of that.

"Um, Riho? Seriously, what happened yesterday?"

Marie was the only other person Lloyd had seen naked. Unaware of this shared experience, she was worriedly peering into Riho's face. Unable to tell her the truth, Riho just whispered, "Nothing."

Eug came sailing in, white lab coat flapping, smacking on her lollipop.

"Oh, what's going on here? If you're not feeling well, an infusion of those leaves will help. Eat 'em straight, and their poison will make you numb, but steep 'em for three hours and you'll get a potion that'll cure any cold in one shot! They have the power of the world tree, so they're super effective."

"I'll just go prune a bit!" Riho said, eyes turning instantly to gold coins. She dashed out of the room, found the housekeeper in the hall, and ran over to her. "Excuse me? I'd like to do some yard work to pay you back for letting us stay here."

"Oh, Riho! Don't worry, you've done plenty."

"Please! Let me prune!"

Pruning negotiations were getting heated.

"Well, at least she's feeling better... Hopefully she'll be okay."

Riho was really rocketing between greed and girly these days.

"Sorry I'm late! Was helping clean up."

Lloyd had come in just as Riho wrapped up negotiations.

"What's going on? Oh...R-Riho..."

"H-hi...Lloyd..."

"".....................""

Clearly, *something* had happened between them. Rom-com vibes were radiating in all directions.

"Oh, Geez! Seriously, what happened? Master! Masterrrrrrrrr!" Marie started calling for Alka as if she were summoning the police...or maybe like a monster calling more of its pack into battle.

But nobody came.

"Oh, right...she's weakened now. Normally, she shows up even if *don't* call her..."

"We finished our talk ages ago," Eug said, slurping her sucker. "I bet she's hunting some medicine to heal that forehead flick or somethin'. Or gathering weapons and destructive magic stones in case you try and get revenge, Marie!"

"Everyone, cover your butts! Run for it!"

Marie grabbed the hems of her skirt, hoisting them up, and raced off toward the warp gate at full speed, abandoning all notions of elegance. She was only technically a princess.

"Maria—Marie! Sorry, I'm going after her. Choline!"

"Uh, yeah…I wanted to say bye to Merthophan, but—"

"Don't worry, you'll be back here soon enough," Eug assured, not batting an eye. "Oh, and—"

She turned to Lloyd. Flashing her teeth at him, she said, "Can you go find Alka for me? I'm sure she's in the house somewhere."

"Oh, sure!"

"We'll go on ahead… Okay, that takes care of that."

Once she was sure Lloyd was gone, Eug declared her preparations complete and headed toward the gate.

With Marie racing rabbit-like at the fore, the Azami contingent bade their farewells to the villagers and hastily headed through the gate in the forest cave.

"Hmm, no matter how many times we go through it, I'll never get used to this gate thingamajig," Chrome said, like an old man who'd recently bought his first smartphone.

Eug slapped him on the back, grinning.

"Just you wait!" she shouted. "Soon enough, people will be using these gates to get around all over the world!"

"Th-they will?"

"Yup! It'll make the whole world seem a whole lot smaller. Brace yourself!"

Eug seemed supremely confident, but everyone else just seemed floored. Like they couldn't believe that would ever happen.

This reaction just seemed to please her.

"Sure, if it happens too fast, nobody'll be ready. Gotta go one step at a time. Let people know what possibilities science and runes have to offer—and prove the need for 'em."

This last turn of phrase struck Riho as slightly ominous.

However, Eug was busy doing something to the runes around the cave. Seeing her do this, Phyllo asked, "…What are you doing?"

"Mm? Oh, that's a secret," Eug said like a naughty child.

Phyllo looked confused.

Meanwhile, Choline was still upset she hadn't said good-bye to Merthophan. She had her arms crossed, and her head was swaying from side to side.

"But he should have come to see us off himself! Where'd he go? We barely got a chance to talk…"

"You called?"

"Eeep!"

The man she'd just been talking about was suddenly in the frame with her.

He was wearing a straw hat and overalls—typical farmer clothes. He was standing at the back of the group, a bundle wrapped in cloth on one shoulder.

"M-Merthophan?!"

The sudden appearance of her crush rattled Choline, but she wasn't the worst one.

"M-M-M-M— Huh? Why are you— D-d-d-d-did other Kunlun villagers—?!"

Eug. She was clearly yet another person whose entire character changed when she was surprised.

"No, just me. I packed up some daikon radish and onions for Mariauhhh…*Marie*, but saw her running off like a bat out of hell. I ran after her so fast that I forgot to drop my farm tools."

He had a sickle and hoe with him. Eug looked very relieved and was soon back to her old self.

"Just you? Good. Okay…here I am, blowing off the job the villagers asked me to do to see this exhibition match. I was worried they'd caught me already. Thought my flawless plans were sunk before they even began!"

"Oh, sorry…well, I'm not gonna drag you back if you're looking forward to it, but I'd like to head back myself."

Eug winced.

"Sorry, but I closed the gate already. The rune we were using is gone, so it'll be a while."

"Huh?"

"Figured we could all use a break from Alka…I'd love to send you back, I swear! But if it's just you…hmm."

Eug trailed off, thinking.

"Hng," Merthophan said. "I don't want to let those fields go a day without tending them, but…I suppose I'll just have to hope the villagers fill in for me."

He shook his head sadly. Meanwhile, Choline was super pumped.

"W-well, welcome back to Azami! Take your time and enjoy yourself, Merthophan!"

Selen was looking all around, slowly realizing her love was missing.

"W-wait, Sir Lloyd's not here!" she yelled, advancing on Eug.

Eug had been prepared for this one, though.

"Sorry, I left him behind to keep Alka quiet."

"You whaaaaaaaaaaaaaaaaaaat?!"

Selen's screech echoed through the forest, but this was clearly all part of Eug's plans.

"Just for a day, I swear! I rarely get a chance to slack off like this, so let me actually relax for a change."

"…But…without exposure to Master, I'll wither away…"

Phyllo hung her head. Her expression never changed, but the body language was clear.

Hmm?

Riho alone was remembering what Eug had said when they first met.

"Once I accept a job or research project, I can't be still until it's cleared away."

* * *

That phrase was echoing around inside her—a nagging doubt. It rippled through her brain.

She wants to skip out on work and relax? That's the opposite of what she claimed earlier. I mean, she does seem a little flighty. I could see her doing this on a whim...

But Riho's doubts were drowned out by Choline's cheer.

"Right! Well, if you can't go back for now, Merthophan, come on! Let's hit the town!"

Super happy to be with him, the female instructor smiled broadly and grabbed his arm—staking her claim.

"I'm still atoning," he said, taking this all very seriously. "And don't you have to prep for the exhibition match?"

Marie could take a hint, though. She clapped him and Chrome on their shoulders.

"Don't worry about it!" she exclaimed. "Chrome's a nice guy. He'll handle it all."

Chrome sighed. "You two are picking up the tab later," he said.

"No, Chrome, if you need help—"

"That clinches it!" Choline interrupted. "Come on, Merthophan! You said you wanted to see what veggies are hitting Azami, right? Let's go scope out the market! There's shops on the main road and stalls on the South Side!"

She dragged him off. Selen and Phyllo watched them go as if they were wishing a classmate good luck with her date. It definitely was not a look you gave a teacher. Seeing Choline acting like an excited child had made Riho forget all about her nagging doubt.

Chrome's square shoulders were heaving as he stifled a laugh.

Then he stopped, and his hands landed on Selen's and Riho's shoulders. Thick fingers were digging in. No escaping that grip.

Grimly, he growled, "So you've been recruited to help prep the match. That's an order!"

""Uh...""

They both just gaped at him.

"We ended up taking yesterday off, so we barely have any time left. And I'm now down a worker. You're the only people who can fill in. Please—I need your help."

That gleam in his eyes was definitely a threat, not a plea. He bowed his head, but this seemed more like he was about to head-butt them if they disagreed.

"Uh, but I had stuff to sell and people to see…," Riho said, trying to worm out of it.

Chrome wasn't letting her off that easily.

"Finish that up this morning, and come help in the afternoon. You two? Are you free?"

"Anything to help distract from the sadness of Sir Lloyd's absence."

"………Could be a good workout."

With Selen and Phyllo on board, the pressure was really on Riho.

"See? Your classmates are both in! You'll be there, right? You will."

Chrome's grip on her shoulder tightened—adding a literal meaning to peer pressure.

Riho grimaced, but he nodded.

"Fine, fine…," she accepted. "But I'll make Choline pay me back for it later…"

"Allan's moment of glory is approaching tomorrow! Your classmate's moment to shine! Help him out."

"………Allan's *definitely* picking up a few tabs later," Riho grumbled.

Behind them, Eug muttered, "………Mostly according to plan. Not a problem."

The rustling of the leaves drowned out her words, and no one heard them.

Back in Azami, the group scattered in all directions.

Selen and Phyllo had nothing better to do, so they went with Chrome to start prepping for the exhibition match. Merthophan was dragged away by Choline toward the main road—like they were a couple.

Marie muttered something about thinking up a new way to prostrate herself to soothe her master's anger once she recovered from her weakened condition and went back to her shop.

Riho muttered, "What a pain." She was about to leave.

"Where you goin'?" Eug asked.

"I'm gonna cash in these killer piranha bones, then wander around for a bit…and I guess probably help them prep later. You, Eug?"

"Gotta few people to check in on, I suppose. Are you, like, hard up for cash?"

"Uh, no, not really… It's more like old habits die hard at this point. Why?"

"That gauntlet's mithril, right? I was thinking of buying it off you. Obviously, I'd heal the limb underneath pro bono…but no pressure. Just lemme know if you feel like it. Since you're Alka's friend, you can name your price."

"You want my arm?"

"Mithril's a valuable resource. And if your arm's working right, you don't need it, do you?"

A gauntlet, huh?

Something about this felt off to Riho. She elected to avoid answering for now.

"I dunno if being friends with *her* would work for me or against me. Maybe some other time."

Eug didn't press the point. "Cool. Not in a hurry on my end, either. See you around!"

She fluttered her fingers, flicked the sucker to the other end of her mouth, and left.

"…………She can heal me, huh?"

Could dwarves tell the exact condition of the flesh and blood arm underneath? Just by looking? Riho watched Eug go for a moment, then turned and headed for the materials exchange.

Chapter 3

A Major Obstacle: Suppose You Needed to Win a Game of Chess with No Rooks or Bishops

An hour after they'd dispersed, Riho was unable to wipe the smirk from her lips.

"Hot damn! Hot damn! So much moola!"

Her profits from the killer piranha bones had nearly equaled the average monthly income in these parts, and the rush of adrenaline just wasn't going away. Her cheeks were flushed, and her eyes were glistening.

"All that for a day's work… If I could commute to Kunlun…I'd never have to work again. Then again, if these ingredients get that plentiful, the price will drop… Gotta keep the right balance. And figure out where to sell these…"

Riho pulled a pair of white panties out of her pocket. Yes—Riho's used panties, the ones made from the silk of a high-level monster called the *earth spider*. Man, that sounded all kinds of wrong.

She could have sold them with the other stuff but had been too conscious of the crowd around her to risk it.

"I mean, selling my own used panties to the old guy at the exchange shop is just super creepy. Looks bad for all parties. Plus, I gotta go back there in the future…"

On the East Side, the exchange shop would take illegal goods or stolen castle treasures alike—ethics like an old school RPG shop. Those shops in old games would buy anything except key items, which was kinda nuts if you think about it.

They served hard-up citizens, thieves, and soldiers alike, which meant their prices were rock bottom, like, basically a total rip-off... If you didn't want to wind up crying about it later, you had to come in armed with leverage, the latest price lists, and advanced knowledge of supply and demand.

They were a real asset to someone like Riho—which was exactly why she didn't wanna sell them her underwear.

"...........But where *can* I sell 'em?"

There were places for that, but no telling what rumors would start spreading if she sold them to a shop that sketchy.

Giving up, Riho shoved the panties back in her pocket. "Maybe I'll have to unravel them and sell the raw thread...," she muttered.

On the narrow roads near the exchange shop, she bumped into Phyllo's sister, Mena, who waved a hand, calling out to Riho in her usual goofy tone.

"Oh, Riho, what's up? You so hard up for cash, you came to sell your panties to some pervs?"

Riho responded with grim determination.

"It breaks my heart, but I've decided against it. Even I have lines I won't cross."

"...Uh, did I accidentally hit the nail on the head?"

Mena's eyes briefly opened, startled. Riho filled her in—at least, how she'd come to get a new set of clothing in Kunlun. She left out the part where Lloyd saw her naked.

"So I'm still not sure what to do with these..."

"Oh, that would explain it...what a shocking story. Kunlun, huh? The village of legend...where even underwear defies reason. Well? You have a good time?"

She elbowed Riho in the ribs.

"Well," Riho said gravely. "See that building there?"

"Yeah?"

"Even small children can vault into the second-story window."

"Er..."

"And villagers use the roofs as shortcuts, racing around on 'em. Grown-ups and kids alike."

"Uh-huh."

"And this seventy-year-old man climbed into a cannon and shot himself toward a nearby mountain peak."

"Urp..."

"Apparently, it's just another means of transportation to them. Using a human cannon to bring someone a forgotten canteen..."

"Sorry, I've heard enough. Forget I asked."

Mena had gotten a look on her face like she wanted to yell, "Elder abuse!" but Riho hadn't let her get a word in edgewise. Just imagining this sight was bad enough—actually seeing the grinning old man shoot himself across the sky was *far* worse.

Mena was worn out by hearing about this stuff, and Riho was, too, for remembering it. Both let out a long sigh.

"So," Riho said, recovering first. "What brings you here, Mena? Preparing for the exhibition?"

Mena grinned, saluting. "Patrollin'! Guard duty. Makin' extra sure there's no evildoers lurking in the back alleys!"

Riho looked pointedly down at the kebab in Mena's hand. Skewers using fresh seafood or meat direct from the farms were a popular Azami street food.

"...You don't say," she said meaningfully. In so many words, she was saying: "So you're slacking off."

A tough-looking man walked by. He recognized Mena and waved.

"Oh, Mena! Slacking off again? Keep it within reason."

And with that, he walked away.

"..............."

"*Ahem*, so like I said, making sure there's no dangerous criminals around."

"You're the most dangerous criminal in these parts! If slacking every day counts as a crime."

"It isn't every day! Just, like, four times a week. And I do drop in on Rol sometimes."

"...Rol? But she—"

"Sure," Mena said before Riho could finish. "But the way I heard it, she was brainwashed. How can I not feel sorry for her? I mean, she's got no friends."

Rol Calcife.

Once a big sister figure to Riho, she'd rolled in with Mena and Phyllo in tow, trying to steal the Holy Sword. She'd taken extreme actions to do so and tried to burn the Quinone sisters in the process.

However, she never had a clear use for the Holy Sword, just a desperate drive to get her hands on it, and Choline—Rol's former classmate—remained convinced there was someone else in the shadows pulling the reins. She was currently confined to the hospital, partly for her own protection.

"Okay..."

Riho relaxed, relieved Mena wasn't out for revenge. Rol had grown up in the same orphanage as Riho, after all.

Seeing this, Mena pounced. "So what's your connection to her anyway? Sisters?"

"Something like that. Not by blood, but..."

"Ah, so an almost sister."

"Not sure if that's actually a thing? But, well, it's enough that I can *almost* forgive her."

Done teasing Riho for now, Mena grabbed her hand and pulled her in the direction of the hospital.

"Then come on and see her with me! Ya need good company on the road! ...You know, helps heal...blisters?"

"How?! Argh, quit yanking, I'm coming. I was already planning on it anyway..."

Riho was dragged off in the direction of Rol's sickbed.

*   *   *

They arrived at the Azami Kingdom National Hospital.

A big hospital that handled everything, from the colds of ordinary citizens to the fake illnesses of politicians. Her unique circumstances had led to Rol being given a private room here.

"You've been here nearly a month… The bill must be adding up."

"Yeah, it's been that long since the Student Sorcery Tournament. Her injuries should be fully healed, but…"

Riho scowled. Rol wasn't exactly fragile… Was she up to something? She knocked on the door.

"It's me! You decent, Rol?"

There was a pause, then a weak response from within. "Come in."

Riho opened the door and found Rol sitting up in bed, white sheets over her, writing something.

Rol had always been pale, but now she was even paler. She didn't look at all healthy.

"How ya doin', Rol?"

Rol turned slowly toward them, like a machine in need of oil. "Oh, Riho…and Mena."

"Been a while, ex-boss. Whatcha writin'? Diary? Will and testament?"

"Morbid!" Riho yelped. That last joke was a bit much for someone in a hospital.

"I'm writing an exposé on the inner workings of Rokujou," Rol replied.

That sounded like a big deal.

"…I wish I hadn't heard that," Riho said, clutching her forehead.

Rol was still herself, clearly.

As if something had snapped within her, a snakelike smile appeared on Rol's lips, and she began grumbling like she was casting a curse.

"When you think about it, the reason I ended up like this is because they're all rotten to the core. At least the corruption at school was my hard work… Well, claiming that now is pretty pathetic, I admit."

At least she seemed to be aware of her own guilt. Mena highlighted that immediately.

"You? Experiencing regret?! How you've grown, Rol!"

"It's not growth! I just…realized I wasn't always like that. When I stopped fighting so hard to move up, I suddenly felt way better…like I'd detoxed."

Riho remembered the old Rol well.

"You were always a little strict, but you never used to be so obsessed with success."

"Well, I'm certainly not trying to move up in Rokujou anymore. Figured I'd better strike first before those rotten politicians try and do anything to me. I got so much dirt on all of them that I can't narrow it down! Real hard to figure out what would make the biggest splash. I gotta hurt 'em so bad that they can't just make like a lizard and drop their tails."

Rol sounded more like someone going to the weeklies for a quick buck than a proper whistleblower. Maybe the most positive take on it was that she was a self-produced devil.

"Sorry, Riho, your almost sister's still a letdown."

"Yeah… She's fully committed to…whatever this is."

Riho was actually kind of relieved at how little Rol had changed. You couldn't keep her down.

Mena started rummaging in her bag. "I brought you something, Rol."

"This better not be the sticks from the kebabs you ate."

"Course not! You said you were out of shampoo, right? So I brought you some."

She plopped a bottle on the table in front of Rol.

"There you go! It's a double conditioner!"

"So not shampoo?! That's the most important part! You can't condition your hair if you haven't washed it yet!"

Mena assumed a look of profound sadness. "Rol, in the world we live in, you've got to keep it together no matter how dirty you are."

"Don't act like there's some deep meaning behind this!"

Riho put a glass of water in front of her, and Rol chugged it.

"So satisfying!" Mena commented. "You can't resist pouncing on every dumb thing I say. Really makes it worthwhile."

"She's clearly got the best of you, Rol."

Mena was obviously using Rol as a way to cheer herself up. Her eyes parted slightly, looking thoroughly pleased with herself, like she'd accomplished a great deed.

"Now, now, if you're feeling this good, why haven't you checked out yet? The Holy Sword thing's all settled, and I'm sure you can find yourself a job in Azami somewhere. I'll hook you up."

"That'd be nice…"

The Holy Sword. This reminded Riho of a question.

"Right, Rol, you remember anything about the guy who asked you to get the sword?"

Rol thought about this for a moment.

"It's like there's a glaze over everything," she admitted at last. "I *think* it was a man, but… Oh."

"Mm? You remember something?"

"Well," Rol said, not sounding very confident. "I vaguely remember him asking…what he looked like to me."

Mena's eyes snapped open, and she leaned in.

"That matches a string of mysterious incidents in Azami. People going missing."

Rol was somewhat flummoxed by Mena's sudden jump to serious.

"Going missing? How frightening."

"Whoops. Well, glad you survived! Riho, that help you at all?"

"Uh, yeah…what he looked like to you, huh?"

That sounded familiar to her, too.

This was about the elderly man who'd appeared in the depths of the Azami dungeon, alarming even Alka.

He'd eliminated the guardian beast of Kunlun—Vritra—then attempted to bury Alka, and failed. Then Alka had punched him in the guts, catching him off guard, and he'd rolled around wailing, and it had been kinda funny, but if that all hadn't happened—she wasn't sure she would have remembered him. There was something fleeting about his very nature.

If he's involved with this, it's way beyond my power… This is a job for Lloyd and Alka.

She'd had a hunch, but if they were up against that enigmatic man, she couldn't let her guard down for a second. Riho clenched her mechanical hand.

"What?"

"Oh…nothing," she said, smiling absently.

Rol thought of something else. "Wait…there was, like, a strange noise, too."

"What kind?"

"Like…someone slurping on hard candy."

Hard candy. A sucker.

"—gh!"

"What's wrong, Riho?"

Riho felt all the pieces falling into place.

"Well, like that mayor's hair, once it's been yanked, it ain't coming back—so where is it now?"

"I think it's in safekeeping at the Azami castle."

"Okay. Take good care of it."

That elderly man—Sou, was it? What if he'd brainwashed Rol into stealing the sword…? She gave me the mithril arm…since my arm got burned and can't move properly. It had to be a gauntlet type that would fit over that…

Riho looked down at the mechanical arm, flexing it.

It's so bulky, it looks like it's replacing a missing arm. People who didn't know the truth went so far as to start calling me the One-Armed Mercenary. And I never bothered correcting 'em.

The wheels in her brain were whirring now.

"What's up, Riho?" Mena asked, getting worried. "Gonna hook yourself up to Rol's conspiracy and make bank off the Rokujou government?"

"Augh! That would ruin everything! Riho! Don't you dare!"

If it was Eug who wanted the Holy Sword, and she's the dwarf who made this arm…then of course she would know it was a gauntlet. She would have to know what was really going on with the arm underneath it.

Riho was in deep deductive mode, but Rol was in the throes of an equally deep desperation.

If Eug's mixed up in this and helping Sou, then her goal was to weaken Alka…and seize the chance to steal the Holy Sword and release the seal on the prison she called the Last Dungeon.

Riho was so deep in thought that she'd tuned out her surroundings. As Rol wailed, Mena just wound her up still further. Disgraceful.

"Rol, those are the eyes of a determined woman. It was nice knowing you, ex-boss."

"R-Riho! Think again! Earning money that way will just lead to sorrow! This exposé will shake things up and lead to way more moolah and happy endings for all of us!"

She was sort of contradicting herself there. Mena shook her head.

She said she was here to see the exhibition match…and the king will be there… Is she gonna take him hostage? Create a diversion to swipe the Holy Sword? Why?

Riho's lips parted, words leaking out. "I'm overthinking it… Why go to all that trouble…?"

Eug was a dwarf. That was how she'd known this arm was a gauntlet. That's all.

She'd ditched Alka back in Kunlun because she always caused trouble. If she left Lloyd with her, Alka wouldn't complain about it later.

It all made sense. Riho smiled, looking up…and found Rol sobbing, arms around her.

"I know, Riho! Whistleblowing's a far better way to make money! I knew you'd understand! We're still sisters, right?"

"Huh? Uh, sure! What's going on, Rol? Why are we hugging?"

"We can use those funds to go for an even bigger score! With your connections in Azami and mine back in Rokujou, we can do anything! Leave it all to me! I'm a self-produced devil!"

"Uh...Mena?"

"Your almost sister is at it again! I just threatened her a bit, and she almost went mad! She should definitely stay in the hospital awhile longer."

"You were threatening her while I was lost in thought?"

A nurse arrived and dragged Rol off her. Riho and Mena beat a hasty retreat.

Outside the hospital, Mena grinned. "That was fun!" she exclaimed. "Back to the grind. We need to construct the match stage for tomorrow... You're pitching in, right?"

"Uh, right, yeah."

Pushing her doubts to the back of her mind, Riho followed Mena toward the match site.

Maria Stadium.

The king had been so excited by the birth of his daughter that he'd named it after her...the most doting of dads. Said dad was currently being studiously ignored by his daughter.

Memories of the Student Sorcery Tournament were still fresh in the minds of Azami citizens, so when event staff spotted that tournament's victor—Riho—they started cheering.

"You sure are famous," Mena noted. "And I missed the whole thing! Too busy lying in the medical ward."

The staff was gossiping about her, too.

"Isn't that the water mage who was in the finals? Mena, right?"

"Oh, the one who panicked and self-destructed."

"She goofs off most of the time, but she's really cold-blooded, deep down!"

"I know, I know. She totally showed her true self during that battle."

"............Mena..."

"............Let's just go."

They must have looked like players from two rival teams yucking it up between innings.

Trying not to look too embarrassed, they headed to their posts. The two looked up at the stage, grinning at the memories.

The place was swarming with people shoring up the stage itself and erecting protective barriers in front of the stands. Maria Stadium wasn't just for exhibition matches and sorcery tournaments; they also hosted bard or orchestra concerts, or event exhibitor sales booths.

"That's where I fought Lloyd...I was so young back then. Just wanted the money... I dunno what came over me." Mena's voice grew increasingly grim as she went on. "I should never have thought common sense would have any bearing on a kid like that."

"Don't get serious in the middle of a joke, Mena. People might take it out of context."

Frankly, it had sounded more like she'd made a mistake no girl should ever make.

Selen came fluttering down from the sky in front of her.

"I heard the word *Lloyd*!"

She landed with flawless elegance. Riho's grin was more of a twitch.

"Wh-where did you even come from?"

"That watchtower. I was gazing into the distance, imagining Sir Lloyd there."

"Try working."

This rolled off Selen like water off a frog's back. The stalker turned her eyes to her hips.

"Separated by miles, each of us gazing at the sky, thinking of each other—the true joy of a long-distance relationship! Right, Vritra… Huh?"

Selen remembered there was nothing on her hips to speak to. She looked momentarily crestfallen…but, like, only one-hundredth of the pain of being apart from Lloyd.

"That's right! I don't have the belt anymore."

"Huh? Where'd it go? What's up? You done being the Cursed Belt Princess?"

"I am! Now I am frail and weak and cannot survive without Sir Lloyd's protection! Oh, Sir Lloyd! I have abandoned my belt, and I'm ready to abandon so much more! Let's ditch this military school thing and make a home together!"

Surrounded by busy workers, Selen alone was lost in her own rapture. The saddest part was how everyone ignored her—all Azami already knew it was best not to get involved.

"Guess you won't be abandoning the stalker thing, huh…"

"Long-distance relationship, my ass."

Selen ignored her friends. But something square hit the back of her head with the exact sound of a cleanup hitter's home run swing.

Without her cursed belt, the auto-guard no longer activated, and the hit was clean. Selen reeled, fireworks going off in her eyes.

"Who did that?! I could get brain damage!"

"………As if you've never been knocked in the head?"

Phyllo stood calmly behind her, swinging a piece of plywood around.

"No! The only knocking I've done is…getting knocked up after spending a steamy night with Sir Lloyd! Ohh! It is true! The shame is almost too much to bear!"

"Stay still. I'll cast a healing spell."

Being *very* nice, Riho gently touched the back of Selen's head, healing the damage.

Mena seemed surprised to see Phyllo so fired up.

"Yo, Phyllo! I figured you'd be slackin' off with me!"

This older sister set a very poor example.

"......I met someone strong."

"Oh, you get into it at that crazy village?"

"...I could tell their lives were like a war zone. I, too, must get strong enough to bring a demon lord to the brink of death by throwing rocks at it."

"That's...the standard? Geez, I'm glad I didn't go. I'd have come back in a straitjacket."

The more serious Mena was, the wider her smiley eyes opened. If she'd gone to the village, they'd have stayed open so long that she'd have wound up with dry eye.

With Phyllo working so hard, she was soon called away. "Phyllo, take care of this one next?" Everyone was relying on her. The foreman seemed ready to hire her full time.

Mena smiled—for once, sincere.

"All she ever had going for her was an excess of strength. Can't believe she's not only attending school but accepted in the workplace... I owe this to Lloyd."

Selen and Riho nodded.

"Because of Sir Lloyd, the belt's curse was lifted, and the rift between myself and my father was healed. All that's left is marriage!" Selen exclaimed.

"Lloyd helped me patch things up with Rol, too...and quit talking about marriage, m'lady. Do *his* feelings not matter?"

Riho didn't want to let her off the hook just because they were all being sincere.

A cheer went up from the other side of the arena.

Allan was standing at the players' entrance. It seemed like some bigwigs had asked him to be there.

He was like a boxing champ scoping out the ring before the big day. The crowd took his smile as a sign of confidence, but his classmates could tell he was barely keeping it together.

The bigwig…was the king of Azami. He stepped up next to Allan, calling out to the assembled workers.

"Thanks for the hard work, everyone!"

The king's words of praise were met with a roar from every soldier and worker in the arena.

He raised a hand in response and urged Allan to do the same.

"Urp…uh, thanks!"

An even bigger cheer went up.

"The man who took out a dragon with a single blow!"

"He turned a dragon into a pet with his voice alone!"

"He single-handedly saved the day at the Foundation Day Festival!"

"He's friends with every drag queen in Azami!"

"They aren't *just* friends."

The stories were getting a tad embellished, becoming increasingly outlandish—the last one in particular.

At a loss, Allan saw some familiar faces and came running over, clearly hoping they could help.

"G-girls! Help me out here! I'm at my limit! When did I become friends with all the drag queens? And why drag queens?!"

"You sure have moved up in the world."

"Oh, it's the subhuman sipping sweet nectar after riding Lloyd's coattails. What do *you* want?"

"Sucking the sweet nectar of a drag queen? I had no ideaaaa…"

"Phrasing! I'm not sipping or having anything sipped!"

Seeing him distraught, the king called out with an encouraging word.

"Allan, no need to stress it! The outcome of the exhibition match tomorrow is irrelevant! Just get up there and show us what you can do!"

That wasn't what had him on the verge of tears, but…the king's kindness was *also* a source of suffering.

The crowd and the king were definitely not agreeing on this point.

"If he can beat a dragon, he's got this in the bag."

"He'll show those Jiou punks! Don't you dare lose!"

Even friendly matches did tend to wind up like this...

Nearly crushed by the pressure, Allan turned to Chrome for help.

"C-Colonel Chrome!"

"We control the stage but not the audience...unless we plant people in the crowd? Hmm..."

Chrome seemed to have other things on his mind.

"Colonel?"

"Oh, Allan! Don't worry! Threonine and Coba are coming, too! They've become fast friends."

"My father's coming?! Now I have even more to be worried about!"

Threonine had finally begun to acknowledge his son, but if he learned Allan had accidentally earned himself the dragon slayer title (with no truth behind it), there'd be hell to pay. Allan broke into a cold sweat.

"Keep playing the dragon slayer for now...I'll do something in due time."

"You will? If you're lying, you have to swallow a porcupine fish as punishment!"

"Mm...that doesn't seem feasible. Can you make it something easier?"

"So you *are* lying!"

"Look, the king is calling you! Go on, Dragon Slayer Allan!"

Chrome grabbed Allan firmly by the arm and dragged him back to the king's side, like an unruly fan being escorted out by security at a meet-and-greet.

With Hurricane Allan out of the picture, a group of older cadets came running up, out of breath.

"Yo, is Lloyd here? I don't see him around..."

"Oh? You need him for something?" Riho asked.

It was never good when someone flustered was looking for Lloyd. They looked troubled.

"It's about Micona... You know how no one's seen her since, right?"

Micona Zol.

A year ahead of them at the military academy, she'd had it in for Lloyd and his friends.

The reason was...not what it seemed. She'd been harboring a secret crush on Marie, and when she learned Lloyd was staying with her, envy drove her mad.

That weakness had led to her becoming a mutated warrior, harboring the powers of both Abaddon and a treant. She and Lloyd had fought a brutal battle in the depths of the dungeon outside Azami.

Then the mysterious elderly man, Sou, had taken her away with him—and no one had seen her since.

"What about her? Did someone see her?"

He nodded. "It's unconfirmed, but we have reports of sightings of someone who *looked* like her."

"Sightings? Where?" Selen asked.

"Um...inside the palace..."

"Huh? *Inside?!*" Selen found that hard to believe.

But the upperclassmen were all nodding gravely.

"I hope it isn't true myself, but she showed up in the Jiou emperor's entourage, with a hood pulled low over her face—but the signs of her transformation were there. Someone called out to her, but she didn't respond...so they thought it might not be her, but..."

"Wait, then...you're sure now?"

The speaker nodded with grim certainty. The evidence...

"In that bizarre form, with that figure? Who else could it be?"

""""""Oh...""""""

The girls all collectively realized that "figure" meant "boobs" and glared at the lead cadet.

He scratched a cheek, looking extremely shifty.

"Look, it's a fact! I can't ignore her single most defining feature!"

Nobody could argue with this, and their IQs dropped a few points.

Deciding they were getting nowhere, Mena jumped in. "Okay, okay,

I'm a palace soldier so consider this intel reported. You'd better get back to your station."

"You're…Mena, right? They say you seem like a goofball but it's just an act, and when you get serious, your eyes open, and you sound totally different…"

"Yeah, like, you don't need to tell me. Get back to your post."

Her eyes opened enough to glint like daggers.

This seemed to make them fear the heavens above. The cadets turned to run.

"Wait," Riho yelled. "What will you do if it is her? Throw her in a jail cell?"

The lead shook his head slowly.

"No…we share the blame for her getting driven so far off the deep end, she transformed herself. We let her drag us along. We never tried to stop her, never tried to help her with whatever was bothering her. If we'd done that, that tragedy might never have happened."

"Well, good." Riho looked relieved. She really didn't like it when friends turned on each other. "Let us know if you see her again—Lloyd will be more use there than Allan, despite what they're saying about him."

The older cadets nodded and left the arena.

Once they were gone, Phyllo muttered, "…Boobs aren't decisive evidence."

This was a fair point.

"I know!" Selen yelled. "Men are trash! Identifying girls by their boobs… Sir Lloyd would never!"

Selen was in full "Not my boyfriend!" mode, but maybe she should wait until they were dating.

While they screeched away, Riho alone was lost in silence.

"……That man took Micona away. If she's back…"

It couldn't mean anything good. She ran back over the rest of the evidence:

Sou was trying to kill Alka and get the Holy Sword.

The Holy Sword was the key to releasing the Last Dungeon, freeing the demon lords within.

Eug might have cut off Alka's power and deliberately left Lloyd behind in Kunlun.

Sou had kidnapped Micona, but someone like her was in the Jiou entourage. And…

Rol implied a link between Sou and Eug!

Eug had said she was looking forward to the exhibition match between Azami and Jiou. A competition with the king in attendance.

Is…that man disguised as the emperor of Jiou?

Everyone saw him as something else, and no one could be sure of his true appearance—perhaps he could pull that off. But once again, Riho convinced herself this was ridiculous.

I've got no proof. Rol mentioned someone slurping on candy, but she could be wrong about that noise. And if I said the Jiou emperor might be fake, and I'm wrong? What then? Can I really propose we cancel the exhibition match?

Riho had her head in her hands, fretting.

"…What's wrong? Upset because your boobs aren't as big?"

Phyllo's guess was infuriatingly off-base.

"Of course not!" Riho snapped. "Augh, forget it…"

The rhythm of their usual squabbles banished all worries from her mind. She convinced herself she was just overthinking things.

Selen frowned at her. "Are you hiding something, Riho?"

"Uh, huh?" The girl looked a little rattled.

Selen scratched a cheek bashfully. "We may not have known each other long, but I believe I've learned to read you a little. You're hiding something—and not a dubious scheme, but something you're worried about."

"…………"

"I don't know what I can do without my belt, but sometimes it's better to talk about these things?"

Riho had not expected genuine concern from Selen. She grinned.

"Heh-heh, you sound like Lloyd," she said.

Selen smiled back at her.

Then Chrome appeared, looking grim. "Why are you standing around talking? Get back to work or we'll never be ready in time!"

He looked utterly worn out.

"......Colonel Chrome, have you lost weight?"

"Probably! I would never have imagined getting a crowd together would be so much work. Maybe I should just fill the place with shills..."

Riho put a hand on his shoulder, looking sorry. "I hate to bug you while you've got it rough," she started. "But there might be something even worse going down."

"...What do you mean, Riho Flavin? Is this your fault?"

"No—I'm not to blame this time. And this is still a *big* maybe."

"Uh-oh. Right, lay it on me."

Chrome was really rattled now. The king appeared behind him.

"Chrome, it's time for our meeting..."

"Oh, yeah, sorry. You girls get to work...hng?"

Riho was standing right in front of the king. That same indomitable grin on her lips.

"Oh? What, you'd like to shake my hand?"

"No, Your Majesty. I've got a hot tip that just might save Azami from certain doom."

"What is it?"

Riho made up her mind.

"Can we cancel this exhibition match?"

"Er, hey! Riho Flavin! Where'd that come from?!" Chrome grabbed her shoulder, but she shook him off.

"Something real bad might be going on here!" she insisted desperately. "The Jiou emperor's a fake and plotting to do something during the match!"

"W-wait!" Chrome roared. "The whole point of this match is to demonstrate that our two countries are at peace! And you say Jiou are fakes? If you're wrong about that, there'll be hell to pay!"

Riho stood her ground, kept her gaze on the king.

"If nothing comes of it, great," she said. "That's better than something preventable happening."

The king stroked his chin, looking her over. "What's your name?"

"Riho…Riho Flavin. I'm a new cadet this year."

"If you're so sure, you must have proof."

Proof…was the one thing she didn't have.

This was all conjecture; guesses based on circumstantial evidence. And she wasn't even sure what they were really after.

When Riho hesitated, Selen stepped in.

"Your Majesty, I'm Selen Hemein, another cadet! Riho may look like a bandit, but deep down, she's really nice! She would never suggest canceling the match without good reason! Would you at least hear her out?"

"…Riho…is a good girl."

This show of support left Riho misty-eyed.

"Y-you haven't even heard what I've got to say yet," she stammered.

"Don't need to."

"…Uh-huh."

"Geez…" Riho shook her head but clearly felt much better. She turned back to the king, grinning once again.

"Proof and reasoning are hard to explain here—it involves stuff from fairy tales, and some urban legends about a man going around asking people what they see him as."

Riho bowed her head. Selen and Phyllo bowed theirs, too.

"Urban legends?" Chrome repeated. He remembered something Merthophan had mentioned back in Kunlun.

About a man who'd said that same thing, and the demon lord's appearance that had resulted from it.

"Chrome, should I believe these girls?" the king asked.

Chrome scratched his cheeks. "...I trust all three of them," he offered. "They're good students, and I'm proud of them. And..."

"And what?"

"Your Majesty, they're all friends with Princess Maria, too."

"You should have said that first! To hell with this meeting! What's going on here? Tell me all the details, and if you could give some updates on what Maria's been up to..."

"""" .... """"

Instant trust.

They'd entirely forgotten Marie was really the princess. That made this whole conversation seem like a farce, and for a moment, they were all at a loss for words.

"Man, you should have started with that," Mena said. "I was enjoying the show myself—only reason I didn't say anything!"

"Also, I'm your immediate supervisor—you probably should have run this by me first," Chrome growled. "Going straight to the king with it? Are you trying to give me an ulcer? I have a hunch you know what you're talking about, so I backed you up, but don't expect that again."

"""" .... """"

Perhaps all of them should have been clearer from the start. It would have saved a lot of trouble.

The king himself had utter faith in any friend of his daughter's.

"You know, all of this seemed odd from the get-go!" he exclaimed. "The Jiou emissary was a very strange man, and the emperor refuses to come out of his room—if he's fake, that explains it! But if we cancel the match outright, it'll give them a diplomatic advantage... We might be better off letting them make their play."

He was a little too committed to this, already entirely convinced the Jiou emperor was fake. However, it did seem like he'd already had suspicions.

"This is hardly the place for this discussion. Let's repair to a meeting room, have some tea, and go over it in detail."

The king turned dramatically, leading the way.

"Hopefully this means we can at least avoid the worst outcome...," Riho muttered.

They were up against an enigmatic mystery man and his pet monster—and without Alka or Lloyd.

However, Riho wasn't frightened by that prospect.

"Even if we ain't as strong, we don't know what we can do unless we try."

She had a vivid image of a boy with a gentle smile, who always approached every fight like his greatest challenge—oblivious to his true power.

That evening, in a guest room in the castle in Azami...the Jiou emperor was relaxing with his attendant. They were, in fact, Sou and Shouma, in disguise.

Neither spared a thought to their ruse being discovered. Perhaps they simply didn't think it would matter if it was.

Shouma took a sip of tea and grimaced. "So bitter! I got carried away and put too many tea leaves in. Seems like good stuff, and it's free, so... who wouldn't?"

Not one to ever regret an action.

"Oh? Is it bad?" Sou asked, taking a sip. It seemed like he could detect neither flavor nor temperature.

"It's not undrinkable, but definitely not good. I bet there's a better way to brew it."

There was a knock at the door.

"Mm? We said we weren't feeling well, and they shouldn't send us any food... Maybe they just couldn't give it up? Such passion!"

His machine-gun volley of words was interrupted by a voice outside the door.

"It's me," said the girl in the white lab coat—Eug.

"Oh, Eug! Is it safe to assume your plan succeeded? You've got the chief trapped in Kunlun? Such passion! Even the priestess of salvation—"

"Is this going to go on awhile?" Eug said, interrupting Shouma again. "If it is, I might just make you give *it* back."

"Oh, don't be like that!" Shouma cried, dejected.

Sou gazed at Eug, his expression—well, it was difficult to tell if he was smiling or not.

"Doctor, your results?"

"It went well! As you can see, Vritra's sealed away. Alka's power drastically reduced."

"Ah! Splendid. I can avoid getting punched in the belly this time."

Sou was a man of few expressions, but this time, he visibly winced, rubbing his stomach.

"If *you're* grimacing, it must have really hurt!"

"It totally did, Dr. Eug! Sou was so sure he'd won, he totally let his guard down, and the chief unleashed one hell of a right hook square in his guts!"

"I never imagined Vritra's skin would be so close by...or transformed into a belt."

While they discussed their failures, Eug settled down on the couch.

"Well, Vritra himself is sealed," she said, highly confident. "And I closed the gate to Kunlun. No mishaps here."

She tossed the glowing egg from one hand to the other, grinning.

"See?" Shouma exclaimed, slapping Sou's shoulder. "Even when Grandpa Pyrid was young, it took him two days to get here from Kunlun! We've got plenty of time."

Sou's expression didn't change. He spoke as if questioning himself. "Obtain the Holy Sword, unleash the demon lords, and have the Jiou Empire conquer the world... All to achieve my heart's desire."

Eug leaned forward, her eyes offering a challenge.

"With the world in chaos, to survive the threat of the demon lords, they'll accept the unknown powers I offer without question. It'll go fast. Electricity, gas, running water, the Internet… It should only take three hundred years to get us back to the good times. And we've gotta make it happen."

"Whatever that means, I love it!" Shouma shouted. "Come on, come, come on! Bring the passion! Passion!"

Eug looked annoyed, but he said, "I left Lloyd behind, too. You know, just in case."

"Oh! I thought I'd get to see him again. Shame!"

"Yes—I would have liked to meet him again myself."

Both looked rather dejected. This aroused Eug's curiosity.

"What about that boy has you both so worked up?"

"He will be the hero of the coming age," Sou started quietly. "He will free me from my bonds, in my stead."

"I don't care what happens long as Lloyd becomes a hero and is lauded for it! After all, he's—"

Eug interrupted Shouma's volley of words again. "Is that a long story? I've got far more important matters to discuss."

"Aww. Well, I'll tell you later, then. So? What do *you* wanna talk about?"

Eug pointed to the corner of the room, where Micona, transformed, sat like a puppet with no strings.

"Is that thing doing all right?"

"She's fine, totally fine." Shouma grinned. "Just a bit of shock from her loss to Lloyd last time—hasn't uttered a word since."

"That…sounds like the opposite of fine."

"It's made her far more obedient. And if she proves less than useful, we have plenty of replacements."

"Well, I'll take your word for it. I'm all brains, but physically, nothing more than ordinary—don't you two forget that."

Eug took a deep breath and slowly let it out. She blinked rapidly, like she'd just woken up.

"It all happens tomorrow. Bring your best."

Sou nodded, not batting an eye. "I am aware. Let us be thoroughly evil."

Deep in a dark pit…Alka was hugging her knees to her chest like a little kid, disconsolate.

"…It's all my fault. If only I'd been nicer to Eug, helped out—nothing like this would have happened."

In the gloom, her memories turned to the past—the distant past.

Alka had been a researcher, working toward a grand goal.

Working under her was a friendly girl, Lena Eug…a pushy personality, always a perfectionist.

She never feared failures on the road to success, but sometimes that could go too far and get her criticized.

"If I pitched in and helped her now, that might increase the odds of her succeeding… Logically speaking, that might be my best option."

If it went well, she might not have to leave the villagers or Lloyd, but Alka sighed, burying her face in her knees.

"So why can't I bring myself to help?"

She glared balefully up at the closed door high above her.

"Azami and Jiou hold their exhibition match tomorrow… We only got a day to act. Unless someone finds me soon, we've got no chance."

This was on the outskirts of town—in one of the countless horned rabbit burrows.

Even the villagers never came here without good reason.

"Miracles don't happen every day." Alka sighed. "Oh, the irony of an ex-scientist praying for a miracle…"

She laughed, mocking her own stupidity.

Rumble.

"Huh? Chief! There you are. I've been looking everywhere!"

"Meep!" Alka squeaked, snot flying.

Lloyd had just…popped in the stone door as if he were poking his head over the saloon doors, going, "Ya open?"

"What *are* you doing, Chief? I know you're weak right now, so don't go wandering off!"

"Lloyd! H-how did you—?"

"Mm? Eug said to go look for you, so…?"

Alka knew perfectly well that had just been Eug's excuse to keep Lloyd in Kunlun, so she wanted to know how he'd found her so fast.

When she just gaped up at him in astonishment, he explained.

"Only one of the horned rabbit burrows was sealed, so I thought maybe you'd gotten locked in here somehow."

"Um…that's it? I can't believe you noticed."

"Yes, well…I mean…" Lloyd looked embarrassed. "I've got a lot of memories of this place."

"You do? Here?" Alka looked puzzled. Lloyd was looking even more uncomfortable.

"When I was a kid, I was playing here and fell in a hole. And I couldn't get out, remember? I was crying and everything. But you came and saved me."

"Oh, that's right! You weren't back by dinner, and the whole village went out looking for you. I remember."

That really brought her back.

Pyrid had given him a thorough scolding, and Lloyd had finally started to take his training seriously…

Lloyd nodded, stroking the rock walls, lost in the recollection himself.

"So this was the first place I checked. I knew you were weakened, so when you vanished, I thought you might be stuck here."

"That explains it."

"Heh-heh, we really swapped places, huh?"

He held out his hand, and Alka took it, her cheeks turning red.

She tried to cover it. "You said you've got a lot of memories in here…"
He'd been bawling his eyes out. "You sure it isn't just trauma?"

"No, they're good memories now," he assured her, grinning.

Alka blinked at him, surprised.

"I was so weak back then. But this is where I decided I had to get stronger. That's why it's a good memory—my origin story."

"Your origin?"

"Yes. I always admired the soldier in that novel. And this is where I decided I didn't want to let that end at admiration. I wanted to make him my goal in life. No matter what happens, I remember how I was weak and sobbing down here—and think, I've gotta try harder."

He turned back to Alka, looking sheepish.

"Ah-ha-ha, big talk, I know. I'm still so weak. I wouldn't even be a soldier if it weren't for Allan. I've got a lot more work to do."

Then he grinned, scratching his cheek.

The purity of Lloyd's feelings hit Alka like a bolt from the blue.

He's…strong. Far more so than I've ever been.

Like that, she realized exactly why she didn't want to help Eug. And that realization made her laugh out loud.

"Pfft…ah-ha-ha-ha-ha!"

"Er, Chief?"

"Ah-ha-ha-ha-ha! I finally figured it out! That's why I didn't wanna help her! That's why I was fretting about it!"

Eug couldn't let it end in failure. She couldn't admit her own weakness.

Alka realized that no matter how many centuries passed, Eug would still be a sore loser.

She'd said she was confident. Said the odds were on her side. Yet…

"Even if it does go well and you can control that power, it'll eventually lead to the same fatal error if you don't seriously reflect on yourself."

Lloyd was totally lost, but Alka was still doubled over, laughing.

"Eug, you've already lost this fight. If you can't face your own failures and accept them, you'll never find real success. It'll never amount to anything but a tantalizing dream. Lloyd, you helped me figure that out. Helped stop me from repeating the mistakes of the past."

She gave Lloyd a big hug, like a sister.

"Whoa, Chief! Uh...what's that for?"

Alka held on to him a bit longer, then got to her feet, a gleam in her eye.

"Mm, I think the world is better like it is. Why change it when we're having so much fun?! The world can develop at its own pace, and if it does...then we can try to control that device again."

He had no idea what any of that meant, and the hug had left him with a tinge of embarrassment, but then he remembered he had something to tell her.

"Oh, right! Chief! Bad news. While we were looking for you, the passage to Azami got shut off somehow! We're stuck here."

"Mm, I figured as much... Dammit, Eug."

"Did Eug do that intentionally? Oh no...I need to get back to Azami right away..."

"Mm? Why?"

"Well, I promised Allan I'd be there for his match. I've gotta get to Azami by tomorrow..."

"Ah...that's my Lloyd."

He always put others before himself.

Lloyd's unwavering purity was almost blinding. Alka dusted herself off and climbed up on his back.

"Er, Chief?"

"We can't waste all day in this pit! Let's go consult the others. Come on, get moving!"

She slapped him on the shoulder.

All trace of hesitation was gone.

A few minutes later, they were back in Kunlun.

The villagers were gathered in the same hall they used for parties.

Lloyd had just finished asking for their help. "Any ideas?"

"So...," Grandpa Pyrid said, stroking his chin. "She ditched you here and closed the path behind her, and the chief's teleport spell isn't an option, but you need to get back as fast as you can."

"I promised I'd be there for Allan's match," Lloyd said, quite worked up.

"Huh…," a village youth mumbled, scratching his head. "Then you shouldn't have stayed behind! This is the dude who got you enlisted in the first place, right?"

Lloyd grimaced but soon met the youth's gaze.

"Yeah, this was my blunder. And that's exactly why I want to correct it."

"That's more like it!" the youth cried, grinning. "You used to let stuff like that get you down."

"Then don't bring it up!" Alka snapped. "Lloyd, he's been worried about you ever since you left."

"Hey! Don't tell him that!"

Everyone chuckled.

"Ha-ha-ha! Don't listen to him, Lloyd!" The woodcutter was leaning against the wall, laughing. "This is the chief's fault for losing her powers and falling in a pit."

"Hngg… Dammit, Eug! You've tarnished my reputation!"

Her reputation was in tatters to begin with, so this hadn't really affected it much.

"Lloyd owes this boy?" Pyrid asked, thinking hard. "And it needs to be done by tomorrow evening… We only have a day."

"Running that distance took you two days even when you were young, right, Grandpa? Lloyd, how long did it take you the first time you went to Azami?"

"S-six days. I mean, I did take a few detours to investigate a few things, but…"

"Well, that rules that option out. If only you could fly like the chief! It would only take you, like, twelve hours."

"Hngg…learning that rune is easier said than done. That alone would take more than a few days."

"We've got the mountain-climbing cannon! If we up the power…"

"Still wouldn't cover more than half the distance."

"If it took six days with detours…then maybe three without?"

"It took me two days when I was a young man, but if you ignore mountains and rivers and just cut straight through, you could get there faster…"

Everyone was racking their brains…but most of the ideas were pretty crazy. Lloyd was listening closely to everything, his expression very serious.

He was the weakest one here. What could he actually do?

"Max output on the cannon is about a third of the distance to Azami. Avoiding detours, I can get there twice as fast…if I could soar through the sky—and go as the crow flies to head straight to Azami…"

"Lloyd?"

Lloyd was muttering to himself, like he was meditating.

Then he jumped to his feet.

"…I got it! I can get to Azami in a day!"

"Oh?"

"—Maybe."

Lloyd's dip in confidence caused a new round of laughter.

"Maybe, he says!"

"I'm not sure…but it's worth a shot! I mean, as weak as I am, I *am* a soldier now!"

"Exactly! Getting to Azami in a day is way easier than a wimp like you enlisting!"

"Still, Lloyd, what exactly is your plan?" Alka asked, concerned.

Lloyd grinned at her.

"All of them!"

"Huh?"

"I'm gonna use *all* your ideas!"

The human cannon was set up in the center of the village.

By chanting an explosive spell at the magic stone, it could generate enough power to send someone to the mountain peak, a one-way rope-less ropeway found nowhere else in the world. Not much different from bungee jumping without the bungee cord.

The villagers were raising the cannon's muzzle to the sky. A much higher angle than they used to hit the mountains.

"That should do it... That's the way to Azami, right, Grandpa?"

"The stars are there, and the moon is...mm, perfect."

Once Pyrid had confirmed it, Lloyd clambered inside.

"I know it's a big ask, but thanks for all your help with this!" he said, looking around.

"Ah, don't worry about it!"

"Lloyd, like I said earlier, when you get to Azami, find Eug at the exhibition match, and smash the egg she's got Vritra trapped inside."

"Will do!" Lloyd replied, looking grave. "I still can't believe Eug would do this..."

"Mm. Give her a good scolding for me! But once the egg cracks, I'll be right along to do the same thing myself."

Lloyd nodded once more and looked up at the sky.

"I can do this... The cannon will take me a third of the way; then I can use my *Aero* spell to fly until I run out of magic. And when that happens, I'll run the rest of the way! No detours, no breaks, just going as fast as I can!"

Seeing Lloyd looking determined, Grandpa Pyrid stepped over.

"You ready? Give 'em hell, Lloyd!"

"Will do, Grandpa!"

Lloyd tucked his head down into the cannon. Truly, it was quite the visual.

There was a huge cluster of magic stones at the cannon base. The entire village was pouring magic into them... The cannon itself was turning red like never before.

"We're counting on you, Lloyd! If Sou and Shouma are involved... you've got a better shot than Pyrid or any of the other villagers."

"Huh? Chief? Did you say something?"

"No, never mind. Off you go, my darling!"

"Leave it to me! Do it!"

Ka-booooooooooooooooom.

No sooner had Lloyd said the word than he was rocketing toward the night sky.

"A six-day distance, but the cannon turns it into four!"

Lloyd's whole body was aching, and this high above the clouds, he could barely breathe.

"And using *Aero* to fly will halve that time again! *Aero!*"

Lloyd fired a wind spell behind him. Gale-force winds sliced through the clouds, and the mountains below were suddenly bathed in moonlight. The sudden light woke sleeping birds, who were startled by the rush of winds and took off from their perches.

"Aero! Aero! Aero! Aero!"

Lloyd could see the sky brightening ahead of him along the curve of the horizon. He was flying barely inside the atmosphere.

Far to the east, the sun began to rise.

"What a beautiful sunrise!"

Well, he *was* in the upper atmosphere.

Lloyd couldn't stop to admire the view. He kept his focus, casting *Aero* again and again.

—Seven hours later.

He'd been losing altitude for a while, his chants no longer effective. He adjusted his trajectory, heading for a canal.

A lookout on a boat below saw something that definitely wasn't a bird flying toward him, and he raised his telescope.

"A girl just fell from the sky, Captain!" he squawked.

"Don't be an idiot! That ain't possible! Look again!"

"Sorry, you're right! It's actually a boy!"

"The gender ain't the issue! You ain't gonna see a human fall out of the sky! Gimme that!"

©Nao Watanuki

The captain grabbed the telescope from him, saw Lloyd, and immediately looked grim.

"Sorry. That is a boy."

"Right?!"

Splashhh…

An instant later, the boy fell from the air, landing in the canal with a massive splash.

The impact was so hard that every ship in the canal was rocked around.

"Man! Brace for impact!"

At last, the waves subsided. The captain made sure his ship was intact, then peered over the rail, afraid of what he might see.

"What was that… Was that really a boy?" he muttered.

Bubbles rose to the water's surface…and a moment later, Lloyd came rocketing out of the canal.

""AAAAAAAH!""

The captain and the lookout shrieked, throwing their arms around each other. Lloyd landed on deck, and all eyes clapped to him in utter terror.

Dripping, Lloyd saw them looking and came over.

"Um…"

"I'm sorry! I'm sorry I was ever born!"

"I'll do anything! Just spare my life!"

He was briefly flummoxed by this display but remembered his mission.

"Er, where am I?" he asked.

"Th-the canal near the Rokujou border!"

"Yes!" Lloyd cried, pumping his fist. He caught his breath and gave himself a shake.

His wet clothes were instantly dry. Neither of the crew could believe their eyes.

"Thanks! I'll be on my way…"

"S-sure…"

"Oh, right."

"Eep! Spare us!"

"You shouldn't say you'll do anything so easily. What if I was a bad guy?"

"Uh…sorry?"

"Someone I respect gave me that advice. Ack, I don't have time for this!"

Lloyd did a couple of light stretches, then bent his knees, getting ready to jump.

"I've got the distance down to two days! I've just gotta cover those… with guts!"

He jumped from the ship's deck to the far shore and was gone like the wind.

The force of his leap left the ship rocking once again. The crew stared after him, gaping.

After a long time, the captain said, "That's…the boy from the legend."

"The legend?"

"Yes…you heard about how the canal had dried up, but it suddenly started raining? People from other ships said it was a strange boy that made it rain. The same one that cleared the landslide blocking the road. They say he brings fortune to all who meet him."

"Captain, then…?"

"Yeah—I'm hitting the tracks the moment we get back! Betting my entire wages!"

He put his hands together as if offering up a prayer.

The sun beat down from above.

In the waiting room at Maria Stadium…Allan had finished his warm-up exercises and was sitting in a chair, arms folded.

There was a faint film of sweat on his brow, and he seemed to be meditating—but definitely didn't look confident. That sweat was less from the workout than stress.

Nothing about this felt earned.

Not the dragon slayer title.

Not his friendship with all of Azami's drag queens.

"Which isn't even true!"

And now he had to demonstrate his combat skills in front of a huge crowd and the king himself. That itself wasn't a big deal, but with the stakes raised so high, it could never live up to expectations no matter what he did.

"Arghh… It's all a huge mistake!"

He let out a sigh like a writer right before the release of his new novel.

"What *are* you doing?"

"Augh! Learn to knock!"

"I did knock! You were too busy bellowing to hear!" Riho sighed.

Selen started whispering something to her. The looks Allan was getting were exactly those reserved for a new hire who couldn't seem to handle the most basic of jobs.

"I knew Allan would be…*whisper-whisper.*"

"Yeah, he's such a bad actor…*whisper-whisper.*"

The more they whispered, the more it hurt his feelings.

"What?! If you've got something to say, say it to my face!"

"I said good luck!"

"Liar! Then why whisper?!"

"We're just shy."

"Oh, we know that's not true! Whoever heard of a shy stalker?!"

He looked like he was enjoying bickering with them.

Marie patted him on the shoulder. "Allan…"

"Miss Witch! Please, make them lay off! I'm nervous enough about this match! Yet they don't try to cheer me up! No! They just try and rattle me even more!"

"Try not to die!"

"That's the most nerve-wracking thing anyone's said yet!"

As the girls left, Choline took their place. "C'mon, Allan!"

"Er? Oh, is it time?"

"Yup, you're on. Let's just hope Riho's concerns are unfounded."

"What concerns?"

"Mm? Oh, you know, just the usual dire portents."

"I don't know! Nobody told me! What am I walking into? This is just an exhibition match, right? Oh man, I wanna go home."

Allan was dragged off toward the stage like a suspected criminal being escorted to a holding cell.

The crowd was really going wild.

The stands were packed, and Allan shuddered at the very sight—why such a turnout for a mere exhibition match?

"You said you were hoping for eighty percent capacity, but there's not an empty seat in the house!"

The roar of the crowd hit him like a blow to the gut.

Their stares were like stabs.

Everyone was taking a measure of him—the rumored dragon slayer.

"............"

Beyond that wave of cheers and stares…a hooded woman stood bolt upright on the stage.

Allan had only been told he was facing a Jiou warrior—her skills and fighting style were a mystery.

He could only identify a gender by the swelling at her chest.

"Well, whoever she is, I just gotta fight her."

He hefted his ax and stepped on the stage, feeling himself growing calm.

Allan had won any number of combat tournaments before entering the military academy, so the familiarity helped him focus.

His mind clear, he looked around once more.

At the center of the stands was a balcony.

There sat the rulers of Azami and Jiou, guards at their sides, Chrome included.

If he looked further, he would likely spot his father, Threonine.

Allan decided to peel his eyes off the crowd, focusing his attention on his opponent. He couldn't tell if she was looking at him or had even noticed he was there. She didn't move at all.

"...I feel like we've already met...?"

The sensation nagged at the back of his mind for a moment, but it was soon driven out entirely. The Azami king had risen to his feet, using a magic stone to amplify his voice and address the crowd.

"Everyone! Thank you for waiting! To celebrate peace between Azami and Jiou, we have arranged an exhibition match!"

A bald man slowly stepped onstage. A ref...but he seemed rather burly for that. Allan blinked in surprise, recognizing him.

"Y-you're...the hotel owner?"

"Coba. But today, I'll be the referee. Good luck."

"Th-thanks."

Allan thought it was probably not very professional to have the ref rooting for him, but...

"............"

He was more worried about how unresponsive his opponent was. He tried to get a look under that hood.

"Is there something on her face? Like...armor, or...?"

That would explain why she was standing so stiff. The hood must have been there to disguise the armor—likely aiming for a counter... Allan had fought enough people to be familiar with the tactic.

"A lot less creepy if you know why, huh? If I can knock her out in one hit, that oughta hide my real skills pretty well."

Even in sturdy armor, if he scored a clean hit to the temple, the impact would give her a concussion.

Winning on the first stroke would prevent anyone from realizing he was no dragon slayer. Allan adjusted his grip on his ax.

End this in one!

"Let the match…begin!"

Coba dropped his hand, and the bell in the corner of the ring clanged.

The crowd roared.

Without a trace of fear, Allan launched himself forward.

"Sorry, lady! This battle's already done!"

People moved slowly in armor; a swift strike was the path to victory.

Before Allan could take a second step, the hooded woman vanished without a sound.

His swing's target lost, Allan reeled. "Whoa!"

A shadow appeared above him.

Without a moment for him to process what was happening, the hooded woman's foot dug into his face.

"Bah!"

But Allan was nothing if not tough. He endured, grabbing her ankle…and slamming her onto her back.

There was a thud, and the stage cracked.

"Too hard?"

He was only worried for an instant. She darted back, movements so nimble, he could hardly believe it was the same person.

"What this hell is this? Some sort of custom armor?"

When he'd grabbed her ankle, it had felt springy, like rubber.

On guard, he tried to get a better look at her gear.

Under that hood, he saw…

"Our…military…uniform?"

"Why is a Jiou warrior wearing that?" a voice called from offstage.

"Micona!"

It was one of the older cadets, working security.

"Huh? Micona's from Azami… Why is she fighting for Jiou?"

The hood slid off, and her hideous visage was revealed—Micona was covered in tree roots and a locust's shell.

*   *   *

"What's happening?"

On the balcony seats, the king of Azami calmly addressed the Jiou emperor—Sou.

"She appears to be from Azami," the king observed.

"I'm afraid I was keeping that secret," Sou said, his voice completely guilt-free. "I have a proposal. Will you join forces with Jiou?"

"You mean…more than our current peace entails?"

"Yes—this would be a formal alliance. With the goal of world conquest."

Sou sounded like he was a merchant offering up a deal.

Chrome and the king both got the same impression. They listened carefully.

"Circumstances led this Azami soldier to place herself under me. I have the ability to bring out the latent strength in anyone, be they soldier, civilian, or criminal. I can turn anyone into an obedient weapon."

"A weapon?! She's a human being! My student!" Chrome raged. He stepped toward Sou.

Shouma put a hand up, stopping him. "Love the passion! But you don't want to interrupt this conversation."

"Hngg…I knew you were hiding your skill."

A bead of sweat ran down Chrome's brow.

"Ah, you did notice! Good for you. Make another move, and you'll be outta here."

Sou paid them no attention. His expression never changed.

"The change to their physical capabilities is merely the beginning. To that, I've added the power of the treant—which allows them to siphon their foes' strength. And the sturdy shell comes from Abaddon—I believe you know personally how formidable the locust's power can be."

"Mm, thanks to that demon lord, I spent five years hurting my kingdom and daughter. Not fond memories."

"You can make that power your own, to use at your will. With the combined economic might of our two countries, we can have the entire world in the palms of our hands, not just the continent. What do you say?"

Sou spoke pleasantly, like a clerk explaining the benefits of a product.

The king heard him out and, without a trace of fear, replied, "No, thank you."

"I thought as much," Sou said as if it was a foregone conclusion.

"I aim to be a ruler beloved by his people. I must avoid conflict, or no one will come to my meet-and-greets."

"Meet-and-greets?" Sou asked, baffled. As well he might be—the king had read some strange business book and swallowed it whole.

The king did a magnificent job of ignoring Sou's reaction.

"And if I went to war, I'd never speak to my daughter again. A week or two is bad enough!"

"...I remain curious why a monarch would be holding meet-and-greets, but I knew when we first met that you were a good man."

Sou held a hand up in front of the king's eyes—a hand wreathed with some sinister power.

The king remained unmoved.

His eyes gleamed with unwavering resolve. A blade at his throat or a gun pointed his way would be equally ineffective.

At length, Sou lowered his arm, losing the battle of wills.

"You're not afraid?"

"Five years ago, when the demon lord took possession of me—I was prepared to die. The only thing I fear is becoming a ruler my daughter does not wish me to be."

"That's the answer I expected!" Shouma crowed. "Very passionate!"

"You are a king who values his people," Sou praised. "In which case, I have an alternate proposal."

He raised his hand again, signaling someone in the arena below.

"Negotiations failed, shifting to threats—just as Sou predicted. Hm."

Slurping her sucker, Eug rose from her seat in the stands.

"What's up, Eug? This is the good part!" Riho cried from behind her.

Shpp. Selen and Marie appeared on either side of her.

"......Hmm."

The tension was palpable. Eug glanced at Riho and grinned.

"What's so funny?"

"If you'd worked it out, you should have nabbed me sooner," Eug said. She put her arms behind her back, smirking like your classic detective novel culprit, caught in the act.

"...I knew you were up to something. That's why you left Lloyd and Alka behind..."

"Yup, I made sure they were stuck in Kunlun."

"We've got a pretty good idea what you're up to. You've teamed up with Sou to swipe the Holy Sword and release the Last Dungeon... Your plan beyond that is anyone's guess, but we're not about to let that happen."

There was an audible pop, and Eug pulled the sucker out of her mouth.

"Good work! You're on the money. But you finding out won't change a thing. You don't need me to tell you the difference between Alka, Lloyd, the Kunlun villagers...and you normal humans."

"'Normal humans'?" Marie snapped.

"That's right, Princess," Eug said. "If Alka and Lloyd hadn't come along, your country would already have fallen. Without them here, you don't stand a chance."

"......Tch."

Marie knew only too well how true that was.

Deep down, part of her was still expecting them to show up.

No use daydreaming.

Watching her words sink in, Eug let out a low chuckle. "Ha! Struck a nerve, huh? An ordinary person wielding a cypress stick doesn't stand a chance against a pack of grizzlies. Sit yourselves back down, and watch this match play out."

The dwarf acted like her victory was assured.

"Eug has a point," Selen urged. An unexpected show of support. "We've been backed by Sir Lloyd this whole time."

"S-Selen!" Riho yelped, turning on her. "Whose side are you on?"

"If Sir Lloyd hadn't been there, I'd never have freed myself from the belt's curse. I'd still be glaring balefully at the world from between those straps."

Baleful glares remained a big part of her stalker repertoire, actually.

"That was weirdly normal. Did losing the belt make you sane?"

"Let! Me! Finish!" Selen snapped. "I don't want Sir Lloyd carrying my weight. I want to be someone who stands right there with him. And if we want to earn that right, we've got to thwart your plans today, Eug."

Riho had not seen this coming.

"Huh. Without the belt, you're almost rational!"

"I am *always* rational," Selen emphasized, smiling proudly.

Even Riho had to smile at that.

Phyllo and Marie were grinning, too.

"...I agree. Don't knock the potential...of normal people."

"There you have it! Kinda feel like Selen hogged all the cool to herself, but today's the day we quit piggybacking!"

"...Phrasing."

"Don't interrupt me now, Phyllo! I knew it was a poor choice the moment it left my mouth."

They were all their usual selves once more.

The smile faded from Eug's lips at that sight.

"Well said...but nonetheless frustrating. How about I put it this way?"

Eug pulled out an egg—clearly not the same one she'd put Vritra in. She threw it high in the air above—and a huge swarm of giant locusts came flying out.

The girls all gasped.

"A-Abaddon's locusts?!"

"Yup! Mass-produced the ones that the demon lord unleashed during the Foundation Day Festival. Whoops!"

The dials in Eug's boots whirred into action.

She kicked the ground, landed on the back of a locust, and glanced over her shoulder.

"Right on! My physical abilities ain't so good, but I make up for it with my inventions! You gotta be prepared for every eventuality. Hit 'em with a 'Just as planned!'"

"First locusts, now super jumpy boots," Riho grumbled. "This is gonna be rough."

Eug was in full sermon mode now. "If you get suspicious, take action immediately, Riho. Take that as a little lesson in life."

The locust turned its mandibles to them, preparing to attack.

"What the hell are those?!" Chrome roared, his eyes going wide as a swarm of bugs filled the arena.

"These locusts were Abaddon's minions," Sou explained, as if he were explaining the bonus in a package deal. "Their size is their sole asset, but their combat potential isn't half bad. They are especially effective in situations where ordinary civilians can be counted on to panic."

The locusts were lunging at the crowd, mandibles chattering, wings whirring, threatening all in the arena.

"I knew you were a good king and would refuse my offer. So consider this a threat. A king such as yourself will protect his people, yes? If you wish to see this audience leave here alive, you will do as you're told."

Surrender seemed the only option.

But the king's resolve never wavered. His gaze remained fixed on the stands below.

"Take action immediately, huh?" Riho muttered to no one in particular.

On the locust above, Eug waved a hand triumphantly. "You may have wanted to smash this egg, but tough luck! Normal humans don't stand a chance against these things."

It was like an older kid playing keep-away with a younger one. Instead of getting angry, Riho…

"Heh-heh-heh."

…Just started chuckling.

Eug must have assumed she was faking it, because her confidence never wavered.

"Laugh away!" she shouted grandly. "Bluffs aren't gonna save you now."

"Eug, what makes you think I haven't already taken action?"

"Mm? Augh!"

Riho's grin was sinister enough to send a chill down anyone's spine. Eug stared at her, confused—and then there was someone behind her.

Smacking Eug's locust with a lightning spell.

Legs smoking, the locust lost its balance, crashing headfirst into the ground below. Eug had to grab on tight to avoid being flung off. The desperate actions of someone entirely unprepared for this eventuality.

"F-fah! Fah! Wh-who are you?"

"Hi! I'm the self-produced devil!"

At the source of the lightning…emerging from the smoke cloud, a wicked grin on her face, was Rol Calcife.

"I gave you the mithril…"

"Yeah, I'm Rol, the one you tricked into aiding your horrible schemes. And I'm gonna pay you back for that. With interest."

Eug frantically leaped to another locust. Once safely aboard, she seemed to collect herself.

"I see, I see—you're how they figured out I was involved!" She was grinning again. "But you're their only ringer? Too little, too late. We've got a whole crowd worth of hostages. You're just gonna let all these helpless civilians fend for themselves?"

A logical argument.

"Heh-heh-heh, Rol's definitely the only one here who would abandon a helpless civilian," Riho said.

"And proud of it!"

"You really shouldn't be…"

Eug frowned, rolling her lollipop over her tongue. She didn't think they should be joking around here.

"…What are you up to?" she asked. "I don't see any way you can possibly cover a crowd of this size."

"For all your talk of perfection, you sure get stuck on preconceptions!" Marie argued behind Eug. It was her turn to act triumphant. "That reminds me of Alka! In a weird way."

"I am nothing like *her*! Preconceptions?"

"………Evacuating a crowd this large would be hard. But…"

Phyllo slowly raised her arms, preparing for combat.

"……What if…………they weren't just any old crowd?"

"Huh?" Eug blinked at her.

A moment later, Chrome's bellow echoed through the arena.

"Everyone! Combat positions! Per your briefings, Jiou is invading!"

In response…the entire arena shook.

""""""""""""""""Aye-aye, sir!!!!!!!!!!!"""""""""""""""""

"Er? Huh? Whaaat?"

Every single audience member had pulled out a weapon. Eug gaped at them like she'd received the shock of a lifetime.

No one would expect the audience to come armed.

Sou and the king were watching this unfold from up high.

This was why the king had remained unperturbed in the face of Sou's threats.

"What is the meaning of this?" Sou asked, his voice betraying no emotion.

"I'm afraid it won't be that easy. Not with my citizens…no…" The king grinned. "My army. And an assortment of adventurers."

"Adven… You mean? Tch! All of them? You planned ahead!" Rattled, Shouma leaned over the rail, his gaze scanning the arena.

"Thankfully, we worked it out before tickets went on sale," Chrome explained. "The expense was considerable…but seeing that look on your face makes it all worthwhile."

"I love it!" Shouma cried, eyes sparkling. "Such passion! They're all soldiers, mercenaries, and adventurers? Allan didn't betray a hint of it, so I never suspected! What a marvelous actor!"

A silver-haired man stepped up from the back.

"We had a particularly bright cadet this year," he said. "Perhaps she's a bit too focused on money, but she'll be a good soldier nonetheless."

"I know you…"

It was Merthophan—dressed down in a shirt and canvas pants.

"You remember me, I gather? This is not our first meeting, merchant."

"Oh…the patriotic soldier."

Merthophan's gaze never left Sou's face. "Merthophan Dextro. Thanks to you, no longer a colonel. Now I grow wheat and onions. I'm thinking about branching out into tomatoes."

Shouma waved a hand, frustrated by this irrelevant introduction.

"It's certainly a passionate twist," he said. "But you showing up alone isn't gonna change a thing."

Shouma was a Kunlun villager. He normally kept his true strength hidden, but now he let it fly—emitting pressure several times greater than Lloyd's, and far more hostile.

"Guh…" Chrome swayed on his feet, feeling like he was teetering on the edge of a cliff. The king felt as if his very skin was bubbling.

"See? I wouldn't lie to you. You'd best do as you're told."

However, Merthophan did not appear at all intimidated. He stepped toward Shouma with the utmost confidence.

"...You're a bold one."

"I've faced pressure like this on a daily basis for the last few months. It'll take more than that to faze me, Shouma."

"How do you know my name?" Shouma asked, rattled.

"I've heard stories," Merthophan admitted.

That seemed to connect the dots.

"I heard a city guy was staying back home... Is that you?"

Merthophan smiled and reached behind his back—like he was going for a weapon.

"You said my appearance wouldn't change anything. Well, I only know how to do one thing."

Merthophan produced his weapon—a hoe, designed for fieldwork. "And that's to plow!"

"Huh? A hoe?"

Shouma was thoroughly confused now. Who held up a farm tool and threatened to plow their foes?

"Chrome! Get the king to safety. Hahhhhh!"

Merthophan put his back into a powerful downward swing...of his hoe.

The impact demolished the balcony, sending Shouma and Sou flying through the air.

All three men fell several yards, landing upright with ease.

Merthophan pulled out a large sickle, as if he were preparing to harvest some rice. Checking the sharpness of the blade, he mumbled, "The villagers said there was a boy who grew bored with the country life and left Kunlun."

"...Ooh... You were there... I thought those were some ominous farm tools," Shouma said.

Merthophan put his tools down and began removing his clothes.

Shouma gaped at him, completely baffled. As well he should be.

"Shouma, I'm gonna teach you the joy of farmwork! Remind you how much better it is than your current misdeeds."

Stripped down to his infamous neck towel and loincloth look, Merthophan hefted the hoe and sickle again. This was certainly a very striking image.

"Hang on! Why strip? Why a loincloth?!"

"The traditional fieldworker style! Shouma, I'm gonna make it so you won't dare breathe a word against farmwork ever again!"

"But it sucks! Not as much as your fashion sense, but it really blows!"

Shouma spent most of his time riling everyone else up, but he was no match for the loincloth man. No one had ever seen him at such a loss.

Utterly ignoring the look on Shouma's face, Merthophan tugged his loincloth higher, speaking with passion.

"And this thing where you use demon lords for nefarious purposes?! I am partially to blame for allowing myself to be possessed. My role in that was a disgrace! But right now, it's *your* roots that need hoeing!"

"Your appearance is the real disgrace," Sou muttered.

These words failed to put a damper on his mood.

"The splendor of farmwork! Let it be carved into your flesh! Prepare to get…cultivated!"

A farmhand's roar.

"Sorry, man," Shouma yelled. "But no ordinary human stands a chance against me!"

And just like that, he was inches from Merthophan. Where he'd stood, the ground had cracked.

This man was from Kunlun—and far stronger than Lloyd.

No ordinary mortal could lift a finger against him.

However, his opponent was Loincloth Merthophan—a man who'd fully adjusted to life in Kunlun.

"I'm gonna knock your head—"

"Rah! Hoe attack! Sickle strike!"

"Whoa?! That was close!"

Shouma barely dodged. One of them cut a gash in the clothes on his chest, just deep enough to draw blood.

How?! Shouma couldn't conceal his shock, but he quickly figured it out.

"Wait, are those both god-class artifacts? And you're dual wielding? That's…not something an ordinary human can do."

"Yeah, these tools were difficult to get to grips with. But I was atoning for my crimes, and the tools came to understand my love for the fields. This is farmwork, boy!"

"*How* is it farmwork?! In what possible way?!"

But Merthophan ignored Shouma's shrieks, expounding on the qualities of his tools like an infomercial.

"This hoe's blade was made from an ancient lithograph, repurposed as a farm tool. It speaks directly to the soul, divine guidance telling you where to strike to plow the fields easily."

The lithograph affixed to the end of it was an artifact called the Tablet of Destinies. This item guaranteed the god who held it control of all things, but it was now in Merthophan's hand, giving him control of the wheat fields. Even if it was the right size, using that artifact for the blade of a hoe was a bit nuts.

"And this sickle is the very blade used to behead a monster with snakes for hair. Perfect for shearing away unwanted weeds."

It was the Adamas Sickle. A blade forged from Adamant, it had been used to behead Medusa herself—a creature that could turn foes to stone if they so much as looked at her. She would likely weep to be treated like a common weed.

Merthophan was done explaining. Shouma, take it away.

"Either one of those should be so powerful, just touching it knocks a normal human off their feet! How are you actually wielding them?! And don't turn them into farm tools!"

"What nonsense… Time to break new ground and teach you the power of agriculture!"

Nothing Shouma said was at all wrong, but Merthophan dismissed it out of hand. Shouma shook his head. They understood each other's words, yet no communication was happening—it was like talking to a drunk. Except this one was drunk on farmwork.

"Need a hand?" Sou asked. He was standing a few yards behind Shouma, arms folded.

Uncharacteristically grim, Shouma shook his head. "You stay out of this one, Sou. I'm starting to get pissed off."

"Hmm."

Shouma spun back toward Merthophan, fixing him with a glare.

"...You talk big, and I admire that passion. I got bored with country life? Please! It's the world we live in that's boring!"

He gritted his teeth, seething with a rage clearly directed as something else entirely.

Let's take a look at the "passionate actor," Allan.

"Huh? What? Invasion?!"

As you can see, he was basically a celebrity on a hidden camera show.

Nobody had told him anything, and he was left gaping at the arena in utter disbelief.

He was starting to recognize a lot of faces in what he'd thought was the audience.

Right next to him, Coba had pulled a mace out of...somewhere and was busy knocking a locust around with it.

"Come on, spring chicken! If you got time to flutter about, you've got time to fight! The realm's under siege!"

"Siege?! Uh, Coba? You knew?!" Allan wailed.

With a mighty roar and a massive swing of his ax, a second man landed beside Coba.

Allan's father, Threonine. He had made a beeline to the center of the fight, clearly not yet ready to cede the limelight to younger men.

He stood back-to-back with Coba, grinning at his son.

"I'm afraid everyone but you knew the truth. You've always been a rotten liar!"

"D-Dad! Argh...I'm the only one left out?!"

Threonine and Coba guffawed loudly. The incident at the hotel seemed to have cleared the air between them. Plus, it was no wonder they got along; they *were* both jocks at heart.

That was when Micona dove in, attacking Allan again. With that exterior shell, even her bare hand was viciously sharp.

Allan managed to raise his ax in time to block the blow to his chin.

The clang was deafening. His hands went numb. If he'd absorbed that head-on... He shuddered at the thought.

"Can't really say you're unarmed! Those hands are deadly weapons!"

Allan swung his ax, holding back nothing—but she had already darted out of reach. Those multicolored wings were letting her fly just above the surface.

"Hang on! Dammit, you *and* these locusts..."

Allan swung wildly, and his sloppiness cost him.

Micona saw her chance and rushed back in.

"...Crap!"

Just as her hand seemed about to drill into his side...

"Micona!"

Someone had called out to her offstage.

For the first time, a glimmer of an expression crossed her face.

A hail of attacks came at her—sword, spear, and arrow.

Her wings whirred, and she evaded them—barely.

Her eyes now locked on her classmates, clustered together, weapons raised.

"Thanks, guys!" Allan called.

"Allan, you mind if we take over this fight?" asked the beady-eyed cadet in front. "Micona, we're sorry. We may have asked too much of you."

Her lips twitched again.

"With *Godspeed* enhancing our abilities and supporting us...you made us all better. But we never even asked what you wanted, never wondered what might be troubling you."

The thing troubling her was her crush on Marie, but Lloyd had stolen Marie's heart, so...frankly, if she had shared, they'd have been at a total loss. That aside...

"For you to turn into this monstrous thing...and say you didn't need us? Well, we're to blame for pushing you that far."

"I know you've pushed us away, but...we still believe that you're our friend."

"So we're gonna defeat the new you and make you take us back!"

"We forgive you for attacking us! So relax, and tell us your problems!"

A touching exchange from the upperclassmen.

A single word escaped Micona's hideous visage. **"Sorry."**

And then she rocketed toward them.

They held their formation, bracing themselves.

"All units! Show Micona what her classmates can do! Prove we can be relied upon!"

""""Aye-aye!""""

He constantly talked about how boring the boonies were and how he was gonna leave one day.

That had been Shouma's life.

The most restless kid in Kunlun, he was rarely at home—always out and about, always poking his nose into things.

Then he grew up. One day, he volunteered to head out of town to do some shopping.

His real purpose? Get out of the boonies.

The world out there was filled with amazing stuff Kunlun couldn't offer.

He really believed that.

It seemed only natural to turn his shopping trip into an extended journey. Carrying his few possessions, Shouma walked on, farther and farther.

A few days into his travels, he rescued a wagon from some bandits.

When he saw it under attack, he got all fired up and jumped in to help without a second thought.

Knowing it might get him killed—but what actually happened seemed to mock those fears.

He just poked the bandits a bit, and they started weeping and apologizing.

It was ridiculous. Absurd. But they seemed to mean it. Shouma was baffled.

While he was scratching his head, a well-dressed young woman emerged from the wagon, eyes sparkling, and thanked him.

In return for saving her, she invited him to her mansion.

It was astonishingly large, with servants everywhere. The room she offered him was enormous.

Shouma felt like he hadn't done anything to deserve this.

When he told her parents his goals—be an adventurer, go to school—they made all the arrangements.

A few days after leaving the village, he'd achieved everything he'd set out to accomplish. He tried to dismiss this as a stroke of luck, but deep down, it didn't sit well—like indigestion.

The school he attended was top tier in every subject…and he was a hick, enrolled because someone had pulled some strings. He wasn't welcomed with open arms.

And yet, he rather enjoyed that.

"Makes it a challenge! Makes me more passionate!"

This is where my adventure begins.

They'd clash at first but learn to trust each other, becoming real friends!

He threw himself into every subject and sport.

Truth be told, he never had to work very long to excel at something.

Nobody could keep up with him—not in studying, or athletic feats…or with the girl's family backing him.

In a matter of days, kids in his grade or above, even the teachers—everyone was bowing their heads to him.

©Nao Watanuki

They were offering up needless praise, calling him a genius, a god reborn.

It felt like they were making fun of him: empty respect, friendship, love—

He was baffled. Of course he was. He hadn't even started trying yet. If he'd put any kind of effort into it, maybe he could have accepted the results. As it was, Shouma didn't feel like he'd accomplished anything. He felt no value in any of this.

He didn't know squat compared to Chief Alka, but they had called him a genius. He couldn't lift a finger against Grandpa Pyrid, but they had called him a living god. It began to creep him out.

And there was one boy who had it in for him.

Heir to a great house, he was engaged to the girl Shouma had saved.

While everyone else put Shouma on a pedestal, only this heir worked to undermine him, trying one dirty trick after another.

Shouma started to like him.

The heir was aware of his own weaknesses and flaws and used his head to compensate for them.

Jealousy was not the best motive, but Shouma started to respect him nonetheless.

But one day, it all stopped. The boy vanished completely.

He asked the girl he'd saved, and she said they'd eliminated his opposition—like she was expecting praise.

Shouma was furious. Why would she do that?

"He worked harder than anyone else here! How does he deserve this?!"

He realized the circle of people around him was claiming he had their backs, using him to their advantage. The night he first noticed that, he went back to Kunlun without a word to anyone.

He picked up the clothes and books the chief had asked for and brought them back home. However, the light in his eyes had gone out.

"The real world sucks."

His passion was gone. The heat had died away. For a time, he lived quietly.

Then one day, he found a boy collapsed at the edge of town.

Lloyd. He'd gone up against the older kids, knowing full well he'd get beat to hell.

They'd sparred for a bit and left Lloyd lying limp. When he saw Shouma looking, he smiled and came running over.

"Shouma! Hi!"

Shouma asked Lloyd why he'd volunteered for a beating.

"Promise you'll keep it secret?" Lloyd asked sheepishly. "You see...I really liked that book you brought back. I thought...I want to be a soldier someday. Promise not to tell anyone! If they find out, everyone will insist I can't do it."

The chief had just asked him to pick up some books. He'd grabbed the book about the soldier at random.

Now that book had given this boy a dream. That fact hit Shouma hard.

His leaving town hadn't been for nothing.

That wasn't the only thing. Lloyd knew he was the weakest kid in town, but he kept on trying—and that reminded him of the rival heir.

"I would...love to be...a hero like the soldier in that novel. Please don't make fun of me."

Shouma threw his arms around Lloyd. "Never! Love your passion, Lloyd!"

The light was back in his eyes.

At the same time, he was afraid—afraid that if Lloyd left town, the same fate would befall him.

Kunlun was where the superhumans lived. What was normal there was nothing like what was normal in the outside world.

People would fear Lloyd. And that might break him.

He might lose his way or feel like everything he did was futile.

Shouma didn't want that. Lloyd's gentle smile had given him hope, and he didn't want to see it fade.

"Such passion…" Shouma felt like he had a new goal in life. He was delighted.

"Passion? Like the fruit? I don't think we have any of those."

"Oh, no, I mean… Lloyd, if you wanna be a hero, you've gotta work for it! I've been out in the real world. I should know!" Shouma clenched his fists, shaking his head.

"Oh? So city life was hard for you?" Lloyd looked spooked.

"Yeah! The world out there is filled with adventurers and monsters who seem ordinary, but they totally outclass me! Especially in the big city…"

The more Shouma told him, the more Lloyd wanted to see the city for himself—and the more off-base his ideas about it got.

Unaware of Shouma's motivations, Lloyd listened to his mostly fabricated adventures, eyes glittering.

"Wow! The city sounds amazing! Gosh! Golly! I can't wait to go!"

Shouma nodded with approval. Then he stood up, his mind decided.

"Love the passion! Keep it up! I'm gonna head out of town for a bit. Got things to do—you hang in there, Lloyd!"

"Will do, Shouma! Good luck!"

The future soldier waved his little hands until Shouma was out of sight.

I'll make Lloyd a hero. That will be my great accomplishment. That will make me feel fulfilled.

He would help that boy earn real trust, respect, and glory.

"Right! I've just gotta give the world some peril! Lloyd only needs the right stage and actors! And monsters—no, demon lords!"

Shouma started working in the shadows.

He met Sou, then Eug—and that led him to this day.

Memories flooding through him, Shouma bit his lip, glaring at Merthophan.

"I finally have a purpose! Passion! So much passion! Goals! Lloyd lit a fire in my frozen heart! This world isn't enough for a Kunlun villager! I'm gonna make his path perilous, so when he's done, he'll be glad he wanted to be a hero, glad he left Kunlun, and confident his efforts panned out! I'm gonna make it so the world will love him for saving it, and that can't happen if it isn't seriously in danger! I won't ever let him feel like I did!"

"I don't follow…but I get that you're passionate about it."

Merthophan adjusted his wedgie. Man, he was the worst.

"Fighting words, loincloth man!"

"You mean, traditional farm wear."

"I seriously don't get you at all, but I ain't backin' down here!"

"Then I'll respond with my passion for farming! Come at me!"

With that, Shouma pounced—moving too fast for the mortal eye to see.

Aiming a karate chop at Merthophan's head, his hand swinging so fast, it sent shock waves through the air.

Merthophan looked right at it, raising his hoe.

"You can see this?"

"Farmers have good eyes!"

More accurately, you wouldn't last long in Kunlun unless you learned to track movements that fast, but if he thought it was just farmwork, let the man dream. Real farmers might be getting irritated at this misrepresentation, though.

"Passionate! Then how's this?"

Shouma jumped backward, unleashing a fire spell.

A massive fireball, so hot it would incinerate anything in its wake.

Merthophan fended this off as well. A single swing of his scythe extinguished the flames.

The way he smugly adjusted the tuck of his loincloth was a far cry from sexy.

"This is the power of agriculture! Adjust your loincloth, and try again!" the former colonel barked.

"Nah, it's the power of those artifacts. Man, you're as bad as any of the villagers…"

The disjointed conversation was really sucking the wind out of his sails. Shouma didn't seem sure how to attack next.

There was an awkward pause.

Then Sou stepped up behind Merthophan.

"You appear to be struggling… This is no time to stand on principle."

"Sou!" Shouma said, but failed to summon the will to stop him.

Sou was now inches from the loincloth man.

"Merthophan, was it? What do I look like to you?"

"Hmm. You were a merchant last time, but now that I look closely, you'd look good holding a plow."

A faint smile appeared on Sou's lips. "You're admirably consistent… When we first met, you were a Jiou-loathing Azami soldier and war hawk. Now you're a Kunlun farmer. Once you set your mind to a thing, you never waver from it. I admire—"

Before Sou could finish, Merthophan's hoe and scythe swung toward him.

"You're wide open!"

"Whoops."

And with that yelp…the scythe sliced Sou in two. He didn't even attempt to dodge.

"…Had we met under other circumstances, I'd have happily taught you how to farm. But as a former soldier of Azami, I cannot allow you to continue your schemes."

The two halves of Sou rolled in different directions. Merthophan looked mournfully down at them.

"I see," Sou stated, his voice entirely unchanged. "I'll have you teach me next time."

"Wh-what?"

Shocked, Merthophan realized there was not a drop of blood on the ground.

He stepped back, on guard…and the upper half of Sou pulled itself over to the lower half. The two halves rejoined.

Sou was whole again. Even his clothing showed no signs of any damage.

"Wh-who are you? Are you even human?"

"Technically, yes. But the circumstances of my birth were unusual… in simple terms…"

Sou dusted himself off.

"I am the hero, Sou. A runeman composed of many elements— including 'hero,' 'human,' and 'immortal.'"

Sou sounded sad, yet happy to be heard—his face looking ready to cry, yet smiling.

"Runes…more ancient wisdom?"

"You've heard of them? That makes this easy. Long ago, during the age of chaos, Alka fashioned me from runes, so that I might provide a ray of hope to guide mankind."

"Uh…"

"I was meant to vanish when the world was saved. But I did not die. A distorted version of my story remained, passed down through generations, binding me to this world, yet with no clear shape. Bound to the concept of 'hero' and unable to change."

This was all so outlandish, it made the mind reel, but the way Sou spoke, it was oddly comforting. Merthophan listened in silence. Was this a by-product of being a runeman?

"As time passed, my presence grew less clear. I became unstable— different people saw me as different things. I can feel pain, but cannot die—a hell without end that one could not begin to call a life."

"If this is all true, then you're the hero who saved the world. Why do this now?"

"Because I wish for an end to my existence. To that end, I decided to kill my maker, Alka, to become the opposite of a hero—to be the bad guy."

He turned his gaze toward Eug, who was straddled on the back of a locust, fighting the girls. That glance seemed significant.

"In the process, I was reunited with Eug and met Shouma...and came to believe that if we made someone else the hero, and I became the root of all evil—I might be able to die."

"And that someone would be Lloyd?" Merthophan asked.

Sou smiled faintly, scratching his head. "Perhaps I have said too much. I should do something evil soon."

He held up a hand, advancing across the pavement in Merthophan's direction.

"An unstable runeman can do many things. For example...touching you with my right hand can cause agonizing pain."

Sou put his hand lightly on Merthophan's left shoulder.

He let out a bloodcurdling scream and collapsed to his knees.

"Grahhhhhh! Wh-what the—?"

His weapons fell from his hands.

Sou calmly made his next attack, as if taking care of paperwork at the office.

"And if I touch you with my left, it will feel so heavy, you are no longer able to move."

Merthophan was clutching his aching shoulder, and Sou put his hand lightly on top of that.

The hand slammed into the ground and did not move again.

"Guh...unh..."

"Finally, my fingertips... Yes, let's say they can knock you back so hard, you'll find yourself lodged in the wall."

Sou tapped his head, and Merthophan went flying into the stands, like an umbrella caught by a gust of wind.

"...You sure are *something*," Shouma praised him.

Sou shrugged and glanced at the clashes unfolding in every inch of Maria Stadium. His eyes surveyed the scene like an orchestra conductor.

"Enough playing around," he said, almost as if he was enjoying this. "The Jiou Empire must take its first step toward unleashing the demon lords and shaking the world to its foundations."

Eug had caught Sou's look. Even as she fought the girls, she grinned.

"Looks like he's done playing and ready for business, huh? Sheesh, took him long enough."

She had her locust darting in all directions, the girls hot on her heels.

Rol was getting frustrated, unable to pin her target down.

"Stop moving! I can't hit the egg like this!"

"Right," Mena said. "Rol, piggyback time! You can carry, like, a hundred people, right?"

"No?! I just left my sickbed! I can't even carry one! Stop being stupid and do your job!"

Mena just kept grinning. "Don't worry. Their strongest fighters are tied up over there. Only a matter of time before we snatch this egg. I seriously didn't expect the loincloth guy to be that good…"

Mena threw up a victory sign…jinxing herself.

"……Mena, look."

"Mm? What, Phyllo?"

Phyllo pointed.

Eug was standing on the locust's back, the lollipop no longer in her mouth. It was now resting on the palm of her hand.

"That was in your mouth!" Selen yelped. "You'll make your hands all sticky!"

Was this any time to care about hygiene? Or manners?

"Oh," Eug said. "This is a magic stone."

"………It is………but what kind?"

Phyllo looked at Rol, who knew the most about these things. Rol frowned, staring up at it.

"Hng…no clue."

"………Useless."

"You're not fit to call yourself headmaster of the Rokujou Sorcery Academy."

The Quinone sisters' withering evaluations left Rol spewing spittle. It had been a few volumes since an exchange like this one...

"Oh, shaddup! Headmasters don't know *everything*!"

"It's bad news, whatever it is," Riho said, sounding concerned. "On your guard!"

"Oh, it's nothing that bad!" Eug said. "I just don't have much magic compared to Alka, so I keep a magic stone in my mouth to charge my reserves. Like a portable battery."

"I...don't know what that is..."

"You will someday! Look forward to it. Once the world has changed..."

Eug fished some sort of seedling out of her pocket, crumbled the magic stone, and scattered the pieces over it.

The fragments of the stone started glowing and were soon absorbed into the seedling.

"That's...a treant!"

"Not just any treant! This is a special seedling, clipped from that girl."

On that last phrase, she glanced at Micona.

As the seedling grew, it took human form.

The face itself was covered in an insectoid shell—too sinister to look human—but the figure took after Micona's. The faithful reproduction of her bust size would certainly delight those with a fetish for that sort of thing.

Then Eug took more seedlings out of her pocket—ten more.

"Uh..."

"Copies of Micona...perfect wooden replicas. Every one as high-spec as the original."

Eug snapped her fingers, and the Micona copies heaved themselves upright, as if they had strings attached. They all lunged at the girls.

Their speed might be zombielike, but their power was clearly a match for Micona's own. Riho blocked a blow with her mithril arm but was flung backward anyway.

"Riho!" Marie yelled.

Watching Riho sail toward the stands, Eug grinned, flashing her canines. "How's that for turned tables? Ready to wrap this up? Time you surrendered and handed over the Holy Sword."

The Micona copies began mowing through the arena.

"Multiple Miconas?! What?!"

"Stand your ground! They're fakes—gah!"

The march of the Micona copies tore through the upperclassmen, interrupting their fight with the real one.

They'd been maintaining a slight advantage, but hit from both sides by separate copies, they were instantly scattered. Coba, Threonine, and the other adventurers had been holding their own against the locust swarm but were unable to withstand the new wave.

"Hngg! Rahhh! You still with me, Your Majesty?"

"Chrome! Forget me! Go and fight! If push comes to shove, my daughter matters more!"

"Your Majesty, that's not an option! Hraghh!"

Chrome was doing his level best to protect the king from flying Micona copy attacks.

They were hitting the adventurers hard. One fell, then another.

At the center of it all, Allan was locked in combat with a locust. A mighty swing of his ax struck the locust's mandibles. He hated fighting monsters but was forcing himself past that, doing his utmost.

"Dammit! The second years! Dad! Colonel! Girls!"

He had his hands full with the locust alone, but then three Micona copies launched themselves at him.

Darting around him, they swung their arms—arms covered in thick shells.

He managed to dodge their attacks. Badly battered adventurers and soldiers cheered him on.

"Get 'em! Don't hold back, Dragon Slayer!"

"Yeah! You're our best chance of getting out of this, Allan!"

"Show us what Azami's strongest fighter can do!"

Hearing their cries, Eug propped herself up on one elbow, sprawled out on the locust's back, grinning as if she were watching a circus act.

"Poor thing! Got that totally unearned rep to deal with."

Allan dodged desperately, putting distance between himself and the copies. Then he swung his ax wide.

"Hnggaaaa!"

A blow designed to send all three flying—and all three dodged easily.

Darting through the air—like flies, impossible to pin down or predict—they soon had Allan surrounded. Their arms swung wildly, raining blows upon him.

"Unh! Gah!"

Allan was made of tough stuff, but this was too much, even for him. Before they could beat him to a pulp, he collapsed.

The dragon slayer had been utterly defeated, unable to lift a finger…

This unseemly defeat led to roars of anger and disappointment.

"The dragon slayer! Going down without a fight?!"

"What the hell? He's a total wimp!"

The crowd's opinion of him was in free fall.

With their greatest hope crushed, the Azami forces began to waver.

"See, see?" Eug egged on triumphantly. "Tear the wrapper off and that's all you got! We got this in the bag, right? Hurry up and surrender, King!"

But then one man got back on his feet.

"I ain't done yet, copies!"

The Micona copies had found new targets but turned at the low growl from behind them.

Allan had blood running from his temples down his nose and dripping off his chin.

As the nearest copy turned, he hit it hard in the neck.

"Arghhhh!"

There was a thunk of an ax hitting wood.

"It snapped?! What?!"

But even with her neck broken, the Micona copy's attacks did not cease. After all, this was just a wooden doll in the shape of Micona—blows fatal to humans were no issue for it.

With its head pointing the wrong way entirely, it swung a fist directly at Allan's face.

Spraying blood, Allan once again fell to the ground, arms splayed.

Kree…kree?

But no sooner was he down than he came springing back up, attacking again.

"Raghhh!"

Another blow slammed into the same spot. Once again, it did nothing, and the Micona copy struck back.

Another hard hit to his face.

With the copy's fist buried in the side of his face, Allan swung, aiming for his opponent's side.

The Micona copy's wings buzzed. It tried to dart backward. Allan didn't miss a beat. He grabbed a fistful of the appendages, dragging the duplicate back to him.

"Get back here!"

Allan swung it by its wings, slamming it to the ground and then raining ax strikes down on its back.

"Yeah! I ain't no dragon slayer!"

Wham!

"I'm a wimpy greenhorn cadet!"

Wham!

"I'm tough, and I don't give up easy, but take that away, and what have I got left? This ugly mug!"

Wham!

"I'm the eldest son of the Lidocaines! Allan Toin Lidocaine!

Wham!

"And I ain't about to let anyone call me ugly!"

Claaaaang!

The last one sounded extra angry.

At the end of this desperate flurry, the Micona copy was no longer moving—and it crumbled to dust.

"Finally took one down... How many left?"

As if sensing danger, the remaining Micona copies surrounded him.

"Heh-heh...I dunno how many I can take, but I'm gonna go for it, Master!"

Allan wiped the blood from his brow, raised his ax, and lowered his center of gravity.

"Come at me! I'm ready! I don't care how many monsters there are, I ain't scared! For the sake of the realm, I'm gonna dust you all!"

"Well said!" cried a voice in the crowd.

Just outside the ring of Micona copies, Coba and Threonine came in swinging.

A moment before, they'd looked too tired to even raise their weapons. Allan was surprised to see them back in the fight.

"D-Dad? Coba! I thought you were down for the count?"

Threonine was breathing heavily. "What dad can rest easy when his son's still fighting?"

"Heh-heh-heh," Coba chuckled, slapping his bald dome. "I was an army man myself... Can't sit idly by while you new cadets are still on your feet. And you really lit a fire under me, Allan."

A roar went up from all around them, as adventurers and soldiers alike got their wind back.

The second-year students staggered back to their feet, forming ranks.

"Are we gonna let that wimpy first-year show us up? Get it together!"

The adventurers were bellowing encouragement at one another, going after the Micona copies again.

"That's right! This pip-squeak can't even drink yet! Can't let him hog all the glory! Or the drinks!"

"Can't just nap on the job like a pet dog, can we? We're getting paid for this!"

"Oh, shut up! You threw in the towel before me! Don't get arrogant now! What guild are you even from?"

"None of your business!"

…Maybe *encouragement* is the wrong word.

Eug scowled at the sight of this. "Why? Everyone's suddenly ready to fight again? Trying to undermine my perfect plan? Rude."

Behind her, Shouma and Sou were talking.

"Such passion! Hate to burst that bubble, but we got shit to do."

"I approve…but drawing this fight out longer would be ill-advised. I'll handle this personally."

"Come on!" Allan roared, oblivious to Sou's approach. "If you can't even take me out, you'll never take Azami! As long as I can still stand, I ain't ever giving up!"

A very, very clichéd line, but his ax backed it up.

As if in answer to his call…the hero who'd saved Allan—and unbeknownst to him, everyone else here—reached the stadium, out of breath and worn out.

"*Hahh…hahh…hahh…sorry I'm late…*"

Like something out of *Run, Melos!*, they could almost hear the uplifting music blasting over them.

Lloyd Belladonna had run from Kunlun to Maria Stadium in a single day.

The first to notice him were the girls, fighting Micona copies by the entrance.

"L-Lloyd!" Marie gasped.

Cries went up. They'd all been waiting for him.

Lloyd politely responded to each of them, and then he bowed his head to Marie.

"Sorry," he apologized. "It's a long story, but I got delayed. I got here as soon as I could."

"D-don't worry! You're here now! And that's all that matters! Thank you!"

"Aww, I just kept my word."

"Your word?"

Lloyd's head snapped up, his eyes gleaming with sincerity. Everyone gulped expectantly.

"Yes...I promised I'd be here for Allan's exhibition match!"

""""Huh?"""""

He was here...for Allan?

He'd seen the state of the stadium and thought the match was still a thing?

After a moment, everyone reached the same conclusion. "Well, it is Lloyd."

"That's my Lloyd!"

"He would say that."

"...Mm."

How easily they give up.

Oblivious to all of this, Lloyd looked around at the arena and the stands.

"Where should I sit? Will any empty seat do?"

Lloyd sat down bolt upright—with locusts and Micona copies buzzing all around.

"Uh, Lloyd," Marie said. "Did you notice what's going on here?"

"Huh? Oh, right. What is this? Some sort of halftime show? Are those cheerleaders?"

The Micona copies certainly were busty, and that would certainly cheer *some* people up but...it would be difficult to pass the giant locusts off as mascots. That proposal would be dropped straight in the shredder at the planning phase.

©Nao Watanuki

Meanwhile, Eug was staring at Lloyd, shaking like a leaf.

"Wh-wh-wha…," she stammered, unable to finish the word.

She settled for the loudest scream of her life. Definitely the type who really can't deal with it if her plans go off the rails.

"Wh-why are *you* here?! How could you make it all this way in a single day?"

"Uh, I flew most of the way and…tried really hard?" Lloyd was very confused, but he did his best to answer Eug's borderline philosophical question. "Uh, first we maxed out the power on the village travel cannon…"

"I don't care! Are you alone? Any other villagers with you? I might have to beat a hasty retreat…"

Lloyd looked rather put out. She'd asked and then refused to hear the answer. However, he was good boy, so he handled it like a grown-up.

"Um, it was only my classmates who were invited here, not the whole village. And I did some crazy stuff to get here."

"Whew, then fine."

The moment she learned no Kunlun villagers were coming, Eug regained her composure. She was definitely one to keep her eye on the bottom line.

There was an awkward silence, and then she turned to Lloyd, speaking in the exaggerated tones of a criminal mastermind.

"So what do you plan to do, Lloyd Belladonna? Are you really just here to cheer on a classmate?"

This reminded him of what Alka had said. His pursed his lips and gave her a very serious look.

"Eug, Chief Alka told me everything. I didn't think you had it in you."

"Huh, that's a surprise… I didn't think she'd ever tell you the truth."

Eug assumed he meant her plan to bring the world to the brink of destruction so she could forcibly advance the level of progress.

"Just because you couldn't revive Vritra, that's no excuse for lying about your plans, pretending you'd succeeded, and then closing the gate so you could flee the scene. That's so sad!"

Lloyd's version caught her off-guard. Completely off-guard.

"Huh?!"

She was left gaping at him. He spoke as if she were a new hire unable to meet expectations and skipping out on assignments to avoid failure—which might work in college but not on the job.

While she blinked at him, Lloyd smoothly transitioned into full-on lecture mode.

"Get it together! Your silly pride won't get you anywhere. If you can't do something, just say so! Because of this, Alka is—"

"W-wait, what?! What are you talking about? None of this is true!"

"What isn't true?"

"I can definitely revive Vritra!"

"Sigh…"

"I just chose not to!"

"………*Sigh.*"

"………Intentionally!"

"………………"

There was a long, awkward silence.

Finally, Lloyd found the right metaphor.

"You sound like a child that forgot to do their homework."

"I feel so defeated! Even though I'm telling the truth!"

She was actually the ringleader! And like Alka, she'd been alive for over a hundred years but found herself getting scolded by a fifteen-year-old.

"It's true!" she wailed, unable to accept this. "It's true! I had a good reason!"

"Which is?"

"I'm going to fill the world with demon lords, start a war, and help human society progress!"

"Are you messing with me?" Lloyd snapped. Not even a moment's hesitation.

Meanwhile, Marie and the girls were all gasping at the scale of her plans, which was the reaction she'd been hoping to get from Lloyd.

Lloyd was positively fuming now.

"I can't believe it! You sound like the villain in a children's book! Nobody actually thinks like that!"

This brutal takedown left Eug clutching her head, curled up on the locust's back.

"Argh, this is the worst conversation! He's too pure! I don't stand a chance!"

"Oh, right!" Marie cried. "Hey, Lloyd, this is such a mess. Eug brought some eggs from the boonies, and because of that, all these weird bugs showed up!"

"Really? This is all Kunlun's fault? Oh! I thought I'd seen these locusts somewhere!"

"That's right! Because of these unhygienic eggs, there are bugs and *E. coli* and pinworms, and it's a whole pandemic! But Eug won't listen to reason! We're at a total loss."

"A-a pandemic?!"

"Yeah, parasites and pinworms and the like...! All caused by that egg!"

"Oooh! And all from my village? Oh, they do look rather treant-like!"

Marie's words clearly made a lot of sense to him. Lloyd basically believed anything Marie said.

"...No, no," Eug argued, but he didn't listen to her.

He was off to the races, putting his own spin on things.

"You know, Alka did say she wanted me to smash that egg. She said it would release the seal on her powers, but I bet she was also worried about the pandemic! Pinworms are the ones that lay eggs in your butthole, right? And Micona was defeated by the pinworms, and that's why there's all these things that look just like her!"

The powerful phrase *defeated by pinworms* exploded through the group, causing every cheek to twitch. City pinworms were clearly some sort of *Alien*-style science horror.

"...No, no," Eug said again.

Lloyd continued to ignore her.

Seeing Lloyd's mind doing unspeakable things to Micona's character, Marie put the final nail in the coffin.

"So we're all busy trying to steal the egg from her! Can you help with that, Lloyd? Otherwise, we won't even get around to Allan's match."

"Oh no! I can't have my village ruining Allan's moment of glory! All right! I'm not sure what use I'll be, but Lloyd Belladonna will help exterminate these nasty bugs!"

"............No, no, no, noooooooo! There's no bugs! No pinworms! Why would you even think that? You ignore everything I say but accept that lady's crazy story without question? I don't understand... aughhh!"

Before Eug could finish her rant, the locust she was riding...tilted.

Lloyd had hefted the front of it as easily as you'd pick up a chair. The locust's powerful mandibles were digging into Lloyd's arm and doing absolutely no damage. Like it was just playfully nibbling him.

"Give it up, Eug! Hand over the egg! It's a health code violation! You're making trouble for the city and the chief! Why are you being so stubborn about this? Are you so desperate to hide your failures? It doesn't make sense!"

Lloyd turned, throwing the locust. Eug went with it, hitting the floor face-first.

"Oww... The other villagers may not be coming, but he's a threat in his own right!" She turned to Sou and Shouma. "Hey! Help me stop him!"

Then she grinned triumphantly. "Ha! Has Alka gone senile? She should never have sent this kid. Pyrid, maybe—he would have stood a chance."

But she was getting ahead of herself.

Shouma and Sou were both helping Eug with the express intention of making Lloyd into a hero.

There was no way either would stop him from saving the day.

""Good luck, Lloyd!""

They waved at Lloyd like parents on field day. Shouma pulled out a palm-sized box with a tube on top—a camera.

"Huh? Hey! What are you— Huh?!"

The unexpected always seemed to obliterate Eug's vocabulary.

"Eug," Sou explained. "I said today was the first step in the Jiou Empire's plans to shake the world but…I'm afraid that was a lie."

"Har?!"

"The hero of the new world, Lloyd Belladonna, arrived just in time to save Azami! His first step! What moment could be more perfect?! Shouma, you have the camera?"

"That I do! Such passion! Lloyd! Eyes over here!" Shouma was practically a photographer at an anime convention now.

"Shouma?! Why are *you* here?" Lloyd said, surprised.

"Hey, Lloyd! What do I look like to you?" Sou asked like this was an inside joke between the two of them.

"Oh! You're the really evil-looking guy!"

"Mm! How wonderful! You will be the new hero in my stead! Keep up the good work!"

Lloyd was unclear why Shouma and Sou were standing shoulder to shoulder, cheering him on. Understandably.

With the backup she'd been counting on out of commission, Eug was ready to pop a vein.

"Right, of course! They only helped me to make Lloyd into a hero! They don't care about progressing the world… Damn you, Alka! That's why you sent him in!"

She ground her teeth together, furious.

Heedless of this, Sou and Shouma had become a director and his assistant, capturing Lloyd from every angle.

"First, we want to pan up, then pull back into a full-body shot. The hero angle."

"Okay! Passionate hero angle coming!"

What exactly *was* a hero angle? Whoops, one of Eug's canines just snapped.

"Goddammit! *I* made that camera!"

Just then, something came whizzing from the stage—right at Lloyd.

"..............."

The real Micona. Her multicolored wings whirring, she lunged right at Lloyd, hand like a dagger.

"Yah—M-Micona?!"

He only just managed to dodge her.

"Th-thank god!" Eug cried, eyes filling with tears. "You came to save me from these idiots, right?!"

Nope. She just really hated Lloyd. Instinctively. See?! She couldn't stop glancing sideways at Marie. Like she was still trying to prove she was better than him.

Following her lead, the puppet copies started clustering around him.

He was surrounded by Miconas.

Lloyd looked grimly from the real one to the copies.

"So this is what happens when you're defeated by city pinworms…"

It was unclear whether she understood how wrong that was, but she reacted with fury. All the Miconas lunged at him.

Phyllo, Riho, and Marie all threw themselves into the fray, defending him.

He called their names, worried.

"We'll take care of them!"

"You go on ahead, Lloyd!"

"……Get the egg, Master."

Mena, Rol, and Selen came after the Micona copies, too.

"Me and Rol can handle these puppets!"

"Heh-heh! The tide's in our favor, and I feel great!"

"Lloyd! Please, save Vritra! This is all I can do to help!"

Lloyd nodded confidently.

"Yes, I wouldn't want any of you touching the egg that caused all this! But I am *very* good at cleaning! Leave that to me!"

Itching to do some housework, Lloyd advanced on Eug.

"Hand over the egg!"

He leaped toward the locust she was riding. She desperately spurred it into flight.

"No! I don't want my flawless plan ruined by this clown!"

"Let go of that egg now! Before the pinworms defeat you, too!"

"They don't even exist!"

The fate of Azami came down to a childish game of tag.

Making full use of her wings, the real Micona had both Riho and Phyllo on the ropes.

Riho was blasting magic with her mithril arm but hadn't landed a single hit.

"Damn! If I just had a little more time to chant or scrawl a sigil!"

Unable to pour enough magic into her attacks, even if she did manage to hit her target, they'd hardly do anything. She was starting to panic.

Marie was also struggling to land a spell.

"If Micona managed to get to Eug, even Lloyd would have to run for it! We've gotta hold her here!

"…Mm."

With Micona making full use of all three dimensions, Phyllo's martial arts couldn't connect. Each swing came up empty, leaving nothing but a whoosh of wind.

Phyllo gave up on chasing her and ran over to Riho.

"What, Phyllo? Got a bright idea?"

Riho looked up hopefully. Phyllo nodded and whispered her idea.

"I think…"

"You think what?"

"…I think Micona has a crush on Marie."

"*Who cares?!*" Riho roared.

Phyllo didn't bat an eye. She never did. Instead, she pointed at Micona.

"................."

Micona had stopped dodging, repeatedly glancing in Marie's direction—like a boy who'd just scored a strike at the bowling alley, checking to see if the girls were impressed.

"...See?"

She was diving close to Marie, then pulling back. Repeatedly. What was it accomplishing?

"Her elbow?"

Each time Micona swooped in, her elbow was grazing Marie's boobs. Riho started laughing, forgetting she was in the middle of a fight.

"Riho! Phyllo! I think Micona might still be in control! We might be able to use that!"

Marie seemed to think this was why Micona wasn't attacking, but it was quite the opposite—because she'd taken leave of her senses, she was sneakily groping Marie's boobs.

"............Get it?"

Riho still found it impossible to care. She rubbed the bridge between her eyes.

"Okay, sure," she said. "But say she does have a crush...what of it?"

That was one possible explanation for Micona's actions, but how would they use that information? To Riho, it was just another distraction.

Phyllo looked her right in the eye and offered a suggestion.

"......We could use Marie as a shield and stop her attacking."

"Be serious. Our problem is we can't hit *her*. We need a way to take her— Wait."

She'd had an idea.

"We don't need to take her down. I mean, she's been brainwashed, right?"

She wasn't like this *normally*. She was being possessed by unnatural influences, barely retaining her base instincts vis-à-vis Marie.

"If we can just free her from the mind control…worth a shot, Phyllo! Buy me some time."

"…………Mm."

Riho made a beeline straight for Marie.

"Eep! Riho?"

Riho grabbed her shoulders. "Listen up, Marie. Say these exact words to Micona."

"To Micona? What do you mean?"

"Don't think about it! Don't you dare act embarrassed or hesitate! Actually, some embarrassment might help."

"Um…that sounds dubious…"

Riho leaned in, whispering in Marie's ear.

"…Can you say that?"

"Why?"

"Please! I don't have the time or inclination to explain!"

"The inclination…? Argh, fine, I'll do it."

Riho gave her a grateful pat on the shoulder.

Very unsure of herself, Marie turned to face Micona.

Micona and Phyllo were going at it. "…Ow," Phyllo muttered. Facing Micona alone was a bit much for her, and she was taking a lot of hits.

A faint frown appeared on her face. She really didn't want to lose here.

But Micona wasn't backing down.

Then Marie's voice cut in. "Micona!"

A quiver ran over her—a moment's hesitation caused by the conflict between her brainwashing and her (carnal) instincts.

That same quiver ran over all the Micona copies. Their movements slowed.

Micona's head turned toward Marie with an audible creak.

Marie took a big breath. "Stop this! This isn't what you really want!"

A faint gasp escaped Micona's lips. "…Ah."

"Shake off this mind control!" Marie cried. "Help us steal the egg! If you do…"

"………Ah."

"I'll give you anything you want!"

Micona's entire body started vibrating. Her hips were writhing.

"…Um, that meant from my shop, right?" Marie said, turning back to Riho.

"Uh, sure," Riho replied, staring into the distance. "Something like that… Wow, so Phyllo's idea was on the money. Yikes, Marie, sucks to be you."

Her monotone suggested she knew something Marie really would be better off not knowing.

"Hold on, Riho, why are you pitying me suddenly? What's so yikes?"

Micona's writing subsided—and she spoke, her voice a hoarse rasp.

"……Anything? Be more specific."

She was demanding details!

"Er, um, like medicine from my shop?"

"And? What else?"

"Uh…tea?"

"Go a little further."

She was really responsive—like she'd already shaken the brainwashing.

Riho felt like the clash between common sense and the lack thereof would probably loop them back around to the start, so she ran over to Micona.

"Micona, listen, 'anything' means you-know-what."

"And by 'you-know-what,' you mean?"

Riho started to panic. *Crap! There must be something that'll pull the wool over her eyes! Something convincing!*

She started rummaging through her pockets like D—raemon in trouble.

Then…she found something in her back pocket. She pulled it out and held it up before Micona's eyes.

"Th-this is…!"

A white scrap of cloth.

Earth spider silk panties, made in Kunlun.

"I'll give you Marie's panties."

"Yyyyyyyyyyyyyyyyyyyyyyessssssss!" *Writhe writhe writhe.*

The noise Micona made was a shriek, a roar, and a bellow all at once. The wings at her back whirred to life, and she shot off in Eug's direction. The panties she'd snatched from Riho clutched tightly in one hand.

There was an uncomfortable silence.

"Does this mean Micona's snapped back to reality? I couldn't hear that last exchange. What did you say? What did you just give her?"

"I…guess that counts?"

It was dubious whether Micona had ever dwelled in reality, but at the very least, the ruse had worked.

Watching Micona rocket toward Eug, Riho muttered grimly, "May she never find out those were mine."

Meanwhile, Eug's panic was reaching new heights.

Lloyd might be the weakest person in Kunlun, but he still had their unique strength.

She'd been counting on Shouma and Sou to counter that, but they'd been instantly reduced to a cameraman and director, filming his every move.

Meanwhile, Allan had gotten the adventurers hyped up…so at the least, it was going to be a while before they could back the king into a corner.

"Why isn't my plan working? You're really pissing me off, Alka!" Eug swore, steering her locust through the air. "But I've still got a swarm of locusts and puppets! If we can take the king hostage…eep!"

"Give me the egg! Before you get pinworms, too!"

"That's not even a possibility! Argh…I've at least gotta stop this kid somehow…"

Then the real Micona swooped in from her blind spot. Clutching a white scrap of cloth in one hand, which was weird, but Eug was delighted! Her backup had arrived!

"Finally! The original Micona should be a match for Lloyd! Get this boy off my back!"

Whoosh. (This was the sound of Micona snatching the egg out of her hands.)

"Huh?" (Eug's face was frozen in a triumphant smirk.)

Toss. (Micona threw the egg in Marie's direction.)

It was over in five seconds.

Thus ended the battle for the egg.

Eug and Lloyd were locked in place.

Finally, Eug let out a shriek. "What are you dooooiiiing?!"

Micona started fidgeting, her eyes locked on Marie. She was totally fishing for a compliment. If she had a tail, she'd be wagging the hell out of it.

Whatever the reason, they'd successfully stolen the egg, so Marie was delighted.

"Hell yeah! We got the egg!"

"If we can get Vritra out of there, Alka will get her power back!"

Riho and Marie were celebrating, but not Phyllo.

"...So we've got it, but now what?" she asked. "Crack it?"

"Y-yeah, I guess so. Phyllo, you're up!"

They handed her the egg, and she unleashed a formidable smash...

"...No dice."

She tried head-butting it, but this was equally ineffective. The shell just wobbled like rubber, absorbing the blow.

"Sorry, but looks like you're not strong enough! Give it here!"

But even with the mithril arm, Vritra's egg remained unfazed.

Eug had almost caught up with them.

"Hate to barge in."

Shpp! Selen had suddenly appeared between Phyllo and Riho.

"S-Selen? Sorry, but this is beyond your—"

Before she could finish, Selen started yelling at the egg.

"Hey, Vritra! Why are you hiding in that egg? We're all in trouble, and it's your fault! Because of you, Sir Lloyd—my precious boy—had to fly all the way back from Kunlun to be by my side! Stop cowering inside that thing and get out here!"

"To be by your side, sure. Hmm?"

The egg in her hand quivered.

".........Is Selen getting through to him?"

"You reject your master's orders?! Fine! Be that way! The penalty will be five nightly reps of Sir Lloyd's physical stats from memory *and* we'll review my full list of seven hundred and thirty reasons why Sir Lloyd is wonderful! Following that, you'll have to draw pictures of Sir Lloyd's face with your eyes closed until you can produce results I deem satisfactory!"

The quivering grew stronger.

"Did I say nightly? That's too far into the future! We'd better start right now! Reason number one! Sir Lloyd's smile is the reason for the prosperity of all mankind! Sir Lloyd is like a sun shining on the hearts of man, the impetus for the creation of new life, the basis for our every action, the antithesis of original sin, and thus I resolve to devote myself to his service no matter how many people call me a stalker, defying the court of public opinion and the long arm of the law, devoting my life and all future reincarnations until death do us part and beyond from good morning to good night everlasting—"

Some of this seemed cribbed from some corporate philosophy speech, but Selen delivered the entire thing without a trace of shame. The people fighting around them were starting to give her looks.

But...it proved super effective.

The quivering turned to shaking...and then there was a crack.

"Aughhhhh! I'm so sorry! Master, I beg forgiveness! No more! Your voice is echoing through my mind! You're still on the first reason, but you've already written enough for a short story! Half of it was just your delusions! If you wrote them all down and published them, the resulting book would be a blunt instrument! You'd have to register it as a lethal weapon!"

With a flurry of apologies, the cursed belt—possessed by Vritra—emerged from the shattered egg.

Eug had been moments from snatching the egg away, but when she saw Selen and the belt, she lost it completely.

"No! No, no, no, no, no, no! This isn't happeniiiiiiing!!!!!"

The loudest shriek of the day so far. She was pounding the locust's back.

"I sealed him! Permanently! There's no way he could ever escape that seal on his own!"

"The results of my education," Selen declared proudly.

"What education?!" Eug yelled. She pointed a finger at Selen. It was shaking. "Anything you taught him! Is absolutely! Fundamentally! Bleghhh!"

Eug let out a yelp of surprise that closely resembled a barf noise.

The air itself began to shake.

"It's them! They're coming!" Eug wailed.

"Oh, the chief? Time to run for it!"

"We've filmed all we can."

Sou and Shouma were still smiling happily.

Meanwhile, a badly battered Allan was leading a desperate fight to save the king from the Micona copies and locusts.

"They're nearly as good as Micona herself!"

"Don't let your guard down, Allan! Leave the root cause of this evil to the girls! We must protect the king!"

"Rahhh! Go on, Allan!"

The crowd of adventurers clashed with their hideous foes, roaring. Allan raised a fist in response.

"Got it! We're fighting to the bitter end, monst— Mm?"

Out of the corner of his eye, Allan saw someone unexpected.

"...Whew! We rush all the way just for a bug hunt?"

That was definitely *not* an adventurer. It was a cheery-looking old man with a cane.

Crap. Has some civilian out for a stroll wandered in here by mistake? Allan broke into a run, calling out, "Old-timer! Look around you! You can't be—"

"Hmm, cities are always bustling! So these are those pesky...city pinworms, was it?"

The old man wasn't making much sense, but he sure seemed super chill about it. Allan decided he'd have to pick the guy up and carry him to safety.

But a giant locust hurled itself at the old man's back.

"Hey! Look out! Run!" Allan shrieked.

The old man slowly raised his head, hand fussing with the scarf around his neck.

"My, what a large locust," he cooed, entirely unbothered. Then he waved the scarf, like he was shooing it away.

"You fool, that won't—"

Whaaammmm! Ka—scruuuuuuunch!!!!

There was a roar, and the sweatcloth shock wave shattered the locust's face and legs, reducing it to dust.

Allan gaped at the dust cloud, his mind locking up completely.

"Uh, huh? Old-timer?"

The old man put the shock wave–producing cloth back around his neck and wandered off.

"Sheesh, such a fuss over a few insects. What is the city coming to?"

Beside him was the kind of middle-aged woman you found on any farm, sweeping the ground with a broom.

"Grandpa Pyrid, don't overdo it! The cleanup's a nightmare."

She was industriously sweeping rubble and half-dead locusts to one side.

"Oh, another one?" she muttered, as if the monster lunging at her were just more trash to pick up. She turned and strolled toward it. "Hup!"

She hefted her broom—and the tip of it was suddenly terrifyingly sharp.

"If you don't keep things spick-and-span, you'll get bugs everywhere!"

She stabbed the locust through the head…and stirred.

Spltt spltt.

When she was sure it wasn't moving, she tossed it to the side of the arena.

"Um? That's…a broom, right?" Allan said, unable to process this transdimensional combat. "Did I…get hit so many times? Am I'm seeing things?"

The sight of this old man and rotund woman cheerily dominating the battlefield was certainly tough to believe.

But before Allan had a chance to recover, a man with a hatchet came tearing through the locusts—wearing black clothes, with a black cloth on his head, looking every bit the part of a ninja.

Shpp! Shpp! Scrunch! Schiing!

He was bounding off walls, floors, rubble, and pillars with dizzying speeds.

"What a relief!" Allan said. "A ninja is much easier on the brain than broom and sweatcloth attacks! Arghhh!"

The very fact that this had been comforting made his head hurt. But ninja were known for combat! Unlike sweatcloths.

Heedless of Allan's reaction, the ninja paused to catch his breath.

"Whew…more of them than I thought! This'll take a while…"

He didn't look pleased by this. He started flashing very ninja-like signs with his hands.

"I wouldn't normally use this on bugs, but…time to make some clones."

The shadow at his feet began to extend…and then grew into a human shape.

"Uh…c-clones?"

In seconds, there were twenty ninjas filling Allan's vision.

This spectacle left Allan reeling, eyes rolling up in his head.

The crowd of ninjas all shouted. """""""""Let's show them what woodcutters can do!"""""""""

"What kind of woodcutter can do that?!" Allan squeaked.

Woodcutters weren't known for cloning themselves.

A mysterious whirlwind appeared in front of the "woodcutters." All the monsters vanished, replaced by an ordinary-looking young man with an ancient sword.

"Are you seriously cloning yourself for these pests?" he asked.

"""""""""Saves time,"""""""""" they chorused.

"Pfft, even this blunt old thing can clear them up. Watch!"

The young man waved the blade in the direction of a distant locust.

"What was it again? Girlsbar? No… Klondikebur? Wait…was I supposed to shout 'Excalibur'?"

As if in response to that last word, the old blade pulsed with light. The distant locust was blown away—taking a chunk of the stadium with it. Pulverized.

"See? All there is to it."

"""""""""Don't demolish the building!"""""""""

"Oh, don't all shout at once. That was just a careless mistake!"

That was way beyond careless! Allan couldn't summon the energy to point this out.

He was just crushed. The adventurers, the soldiers, Coba, and Threonine were all just gaping, unable to believe their eyes.

"What is going on?"

Old-timers, ninjas…and there were some little kids playing with the monsters in the distance.

"Let's see who can throw the bugs the farthest!"

"You're on! I'll go first! Hah! Yikes!"

The second the kid grabbed the locust, its torso collapsed, and limbs flew in all directions.

"Ha-ha! You squeezed too tight! These things are weak, so they turn to dust really easy."

"Aw, what a waste! I saw a bigger one over there. Let's try that!"

"Those are real fragile, too! Careful!"

"These giants are...fragile? What am I? Am I dreaming?"

A tiny little girl came tottering by, white robes flowing—Alka. She went up to the kids and rapped them on their heads.

"Now, now, we're not here to play! Focus on killing all these bugs. Remember what I told you?"

"Sorry, Chief! We'll gather the locusts and human-shaped treants in the center of the arena."

"That's right! It'll be faster if we smash them all at once."

Alka pointed at the stage—which was already teeming with insects and Micona copies. The copies were writhing like broken dolls, and the locusts were futilely mashing their mandibles.

"................."

Unable to speak, Allan looked past the stage—and saw a totally normal-looking farmer waving a hand.

"Chief! We got a bunch rounded up! Ya wanna do the honors?"

Alka gave a satisfied nod. "Mm. Give it some space, everyone!" she called, pointing her fingers at the sky above. "I'll make it the smallest meteorite I can for control... Hmm, pretty good!"

There was an earsplitting roar, and a rock covered in crimson flames smashed into the stage.

"Wh-wh-wh-wh-wh-what was thaaaat?!" Allan screeched. First a sweatcloth that made shock waves, now meteorites?!

©Nao Watanuki

Alka nodded, pleased with the destruction she'd unleashed on monster and stage alike.

"That takes care of that! I've got a few people to say hi to, so I'm gonna bow out early."

"We're done already? Man, I don't see what all the fuss is about. It's just a few bugs!"

"Don't be such a grouch, Grandpa. They don't get bugs like this in the city."

Everyone was laughing like a job well done.

"Yeah, like the chief said, 'City folk're scared of bugs, so they've asked us country folk for help!'"

"Teleporting here through that crystal was way harder than the extermination," grumbled the young man with the old sword—Excalibur. "We smashed the hell out of somebody's house on the way out of that thing... Not my problem!"

""""""""""Don't worry, I fixed it,""""""""""" assured the woodcutter clone crowd.

Everyone else present simply boggled at the sight.

While the Kunlun villagers' attack was giving Allan and the adventurer's jaws a workout, Eug's eyes were ready to pop out of their sockets.

"Kunlun villagers...Alka...urp..."

The locust she'd been riding dissolved to dust, and she fell to the ground. She was left crawling to Alka's feet.

"Shame, Eug. I'm back, as sexy as ever."

Alka struck a pose that was the farthest possible thing from sexy.

"Dammit! We didn't even get the Holy Sword yet!" Eug whined. "My perfect plan..."

"You're always like this! Too confident of your own strategies. If you can't even accept your own weaknesses and grow, you'll never be able to control that thing."

"Shut up! I *will* surpass you! I'm gonna develop this world and prove I can control the Last Dungeon's power!"

Alka looked at Eug like a toddler throwing a tantrum.

"Then I'll oppose you with all my might. I've chosen to let this world take its time. And follow it wherever it might go. I'm not letting you stop me, Eug."

Alka reached out to grab her.

"That, we can't allow, Alka."

"It ain't what I'd call passionate, Chief!"

Sou and Shouma had appeared on either side of Eug.

"You're still here?" Alka growled.

"I'd love to kill you here and now," Sou said. "But today is not the day."

"Really? You're gonna let this chance slip through your fingers?"

"Of course." Sou shrugged. "First, we have to edit Lloyd's exploits! With myself as the villain, and Lloyd as the remarkable hero, leaving undeniable evidence for the world to come."

"Edit? You were filming that?!" Alka balked, blinking at him.

Sou nodded. "You have any idea how long I've been wandering as a runeman? As long as the myths about me linger, I can never truly vanish. This demands hard work! Even a five-minute video deserves at least five hours in the editing booth."

Alka gave him a look reserved for pretentious You—ubers. But a moment later, she was distracted by something much more horrifying.

"Wow, Lloyd! You've grown so strong! The first step to true heroics! Such passion!"

Shouma had his arms around Lloyd, rubbing his head.

"Shouma! What's going on here?"

"Don't worry about a thing, Lloyd! I've gotta go edit all the footage we shot."

Alka gaped at him. "Shouma?!" she shrieked. "Hey! Shouma! What are you *doing*?"

"Just you watch, Chief! I'll do anything for Lloyd! More than you ever could! Just you wait—I'll prove it! Bye!"

Shouma had thoroughly mussed Lloyd's soft hair by now. Alka looked envious.

Clearly, these two were a lot alike.

"You'll die for this!" Alka roared, pouncing like a lion. "Lloyd will never be yours!"

Shouma dodged easily. "I'm not sure what you mean by that!" he shouted. "But he's definitely not yours, either. Also, you're the one who's gonna die. I mean, even if you do, you'll resurrect in, like, a year, right? And it would be good for Sou!"

"Fool! That year is precious! Lloyd's just hitting puberty! A year can make a huge difference in all sorts of places! You've got to examine adolescent boys at least once every three days!"

How proud she was of her crimes.

With Alka clearly not in prime condition, Shouma was easily dodging her and giving Lloyd hugs between evasions. Finally, he reluctantly stepped aside. He and Sou hauled Eug to her feet and leaped backward.

"Let's get outta here, Dr. Eug!"

"Mm, I want to edit this! Loan me your 'con-puter' later."

Under his arm, Eug flailed her arms and legs.

"How dare you! If you'd done your part, this would never have happened!"

"Yeah, but it was the first step toward Lloyd's heroic legend!"

"If the Kunlun villagers hadn't arrived, it would have been perfect... This time, the extras may have cleared things up, but next time, it'll be all Lloyd! Oh, I'm getting heated up just thinking about it!"

An expression of rapture crossed Shouma's face.

"Shouma!" Grandpa Pyrid roared, spying him with Eug and Sou. "I thought I hadn't seen you in a while! What are you wasting your time on now?!"

"Whoops, Grandpa Pyrid... He could be trouble. Let's run for it," Sou said—not exactly answering the question. He opened a teleport gate.

"Dammit! I won't lose next time! Remember that!" Eug barked, hitting all the clichés.

Shouma and Sou stepped through the gate, leaving only their heads and arms poking out so they could wave at Lloyd one last time.

"There you have it, Lloyd! Our passionate brother-ship will go on, I promise!"

"Indeed, Lloyd! I promise to continue to get up to no good!"

"Let's get a move on!" Eug yelled. "Alka! Next time I'll prove how perfect I am! Hey! Watch your hands!"

And they vanished in a puff of farce and fluster.

"Is it...over?" Riho whispered. The tension of mortal combat faded, her knees buckled, and she slumped to the ground.

"The crowd still seemed pretty worked up," Rol pointed out.

"Well, yeah," Mena said, pointing to the cause. "Look there."

"Whatever he's up to, nice to see Shouma again."

"He loves Lloyd as much as Chief Alka, huh?"

"Okay, everyone, enough chitchat."

Right, all the Kunlun villagers were still here.

The fight may have been done, but nobody knew who these people were. It was too early to celebrate. If you've ever read a manga that went on way too long, you'd know ninety-nine percent of the time, people like this turn out to be the next (and far greater) threat.

So the adventurers and soldiers were all bracing themselves, ready for anything. Hands on their weapons, a powder keg ready to go off.

"Chrome, are they our enemies?" the king asked.

"No," Chrome said, picking his words. "I don't think so. They're, uh... How can I put this...?"

He couldn't exactly admit they were from the legendary village of Kunlun. That would require he explain that Lloyd was from there, too.

Choline was busy tending to Merthophan's injuries, but like Chrome, she was wondering what to do next... Before anyone answered, Allan stepped forward.

"I've got a lot of questions here," he said. "Who are you people?"

The crowd around him gulped, in awe of his courage.

"...Allan knows no fear!"

"Can even he survive this?"

"Damn, Allan!"

Hearing this, Grandpa Pyrid crooked an eyebrow.

"Mm? Allan?" he parroted, as if trying to remember something. "Allan... Oh! Ohhhhhh, so you're Allan!"

At this cry of delight, the other villagers remembered the same thing.

"Ah, so this is him!"

"You're the one who helped Lloyd!"

"Oh, my! This boy?"

"Thanks, mister!"

All of them were remembering what Lloyd had said during the banquet: A soldier named Allan had helped him get enlisted. And they were all acting as though they'd just met a celebrity.

"Huh? Huh? What?" Allan sputtered.

Grandpa Pyrid stepped forward with his hand outstretched.

"A pleasure to meet you, Allan!" he cried.

He took Allan's hand, shaking it vigorously.

Allan desperately searched for an explanation.

With no information to base that on, all he could do was stare in shock as a line formed in front of him, villager after villager bowing their heads to him.

""""""Thank you so much, Allan! Keep up the good work!""""""

"Uh, you're welcome?" Allan said, basically on reflex. The villagers seemed thoroughly satisfied with this interaction.

"Right, let's get on home! This way!" Alka called. Following her lead, they all began shuffling out of the stadium.

"Uh, but who are they? I seriously have no idea...," Allan muttered. He turned to the crowd around him, seeking answers.

But the adventurers and soldiers...were staring at him with respect and awe.

"Wow, Allan," someone whispered. "Those powerful warriors work for you?"

This unleashed a chorus of praise.

"So they're the secret to the dragon slayer's strength?"

"If people like that are bowing to him...he must have earned their respect!"

"Perhaps he summoned the ancient heroes!"

"Like *that* matters, tiger! He had *our* respect from day one!"

"I'm sorry if I ever disrespected you, Allan! Lloyd and those villagers...they're all your minions?!"

"Uh...huh? What?"

"You're amazing, Allan."

"C-Colonel Chrome?! Uh...help?"

"I have no idea how to explain any of this, so this is working out perfectly. I promise I'll swallow a porcupine fish later."

"I didn't ask you to! Hey! Listen! I'm not strong at alllllll!"

"We cool with that?"

"Sure, it's hilarious. Let's roll with it."

And thus, the Jiou invasion of Azami resulted in nothing more than the mistaken belief that Allan was a badass.

A few weeks after the Jiou Empire exhibition match-turned-attack...

The military had yet to receive a moment's rest.

The enemy emperor himself had come to Azami to deliver a declaration of war. The friendly relationship between the two countries collapsed; both sides beefed up border security, and the top brass was in meetings from morning to night.

The Jiou Empire seemed to be making its own preparations. There was no sign of them taking any direct actions—like they'd skipped from the outbreak of hostilities right to a cold war.

The cadets had been assigned to turn the empty warehouses on the

South Side into a place to house the refugees fleeing Jiou, unable to accept Sou's plans.

Soldiers carried planks of wood, buffeted by the sea breeze.

Riho was lying on a pile of those planks, staring half-lidded at the clouds drifting by above. Totally slacking off.

"I figured out Jiou's plans first, but do I get any gratitude? Nooo. They just put me to work."

"But you aren't working, Riho!" Selen snapped. She was busy organizing supplies. "Asking for no reward is considered a virtue, you know."

"Virtue, my foot! You need money to live! Ugh, I'm *so* not in the mood."

She reluctantly sat up, watching Selen work. Selen was not actually doing anything herself. She was leaving it all to the straps of her cursed belt, Vritra.

"You seem to be slacking off plenty yourself."

"M-Master, I agree with Riho! I need a little break…" Vritra sounded exhausted.

Selen rejected this proposal out of hand. "Quit your grumbling! I am extremely busy gazing at Sir Lloyd. I'll make up for it by talking to you all night long! Give and take!"

"Can I give up instead?"

Selen's offer was hardly a fair trade.

Selen paid Vritra's protests no heed, her eyes locked on Lloyd. He was really working up a sweat, happily hammering away with a carpenter he knew.

"Oh, Sir Lloyd doing manual labor is a feast for the eyes! Vritra, let's meet our quota for the day. Then I can go stand closer to him!"

"……Perhaps I'd have been better off remaining sealed away, bamboozled by Eug. No—it was my failure that led to this girl losing her childhood. I must persevere! Sigh…"

Vritra set about his task once more.

Lloyd came vaulting over to them, jumping so far, the carpenter fell over in surprise.

"Right! How's it going over here? I've finished up my task, so I can help!"

"Oh, Sir Lloyd! Shall we split up the work here? Vritra, you can take a break now."

Vritra backed away, and Selen happily moved to stand next to Lloyd.

"You're a god, Lloyd!" Vritra whispered, trembling with gratitude.

"You're really fired up about this, Lloyd," Riho observed. "Any reason why?"

"Oh," Lloyd said bashfully. "I just heard the Jiou Empire did something awful while I was running late to the exhibition match. But Allan and Marie took care of it! As a soldier, I wish I'd been there to help…but all I could do was clean up those pinworms. So I wanted to make up for it by helping here!"

He was a huge help, but Lloyd's self-evaluations remained permanently low.

Riho shook her head, but Lloyd looked so serious, she couldn't bring herself to say another word. "Well, that goes for all of us," she managed.

A gang of older cadets came shuffling over to them.

"…………"

Micona was in the lead. She seemed fully recovered, in good health… and was glaring at the boy from Kunlun.

"M-Micona…" Lloyd sounded worried.

"I have something to say to you," she growled. "First…thanks for saving me."

She bowed low.

"And thanks for reminding me how important companions are. On my own, I accomplished absolutely nothing."

Lloyd's group was shocked by this reversal.

He smiled, holding out his hand. "I'm not sure what that means, but here's to working with you in the future."

Micona did not take his hand. Instead, she struck a dramatic pose—which caused quite a bit of jiggle.

"But now! My main point! You'll regret teaching me the importance of friendship! My group originally assembled because we were all extremely competitive! And now we're closer than ever! We're guaranteed to get more acclaim than you ever will! Bow your heads! And one more thing, Lloyd Belladonna!"

"Yes?"

"I will never lose to you. We are rivals till the bitter end—the day I win!"

"...Okay!"

Lloyd smiled happily, and Micona flashed a triumphant grin.

"What say we have a competition here? Second-years versus first-years! Which team can construct the most temporary housing? We've as good as won this already!"

"Oh?"

"With my *Godspeed* heightening our abilities and our newfound unity, it's like we were born to build! A necessary skill for any soldier!"

Maybe if they were talking about digging trenches and making camp.

Micona was oblivious to the disconnect.

"You all have your talents, but your talent for slacking off has sunk in deep, like a sweat stain on your collar. You can never hope to match our pace! Today, or any other!"

At this point, Micona pulled a white cloth out of her pocket and wiped the sweat from her brow.

The pair of Marie's (ostensibly) panties that Riho had given her. Despite the brainwashing, she seemed to have remembered exactly what those were and was making sure they never left her side.

"...I can never tell her the truth."

If Micona found out those panties were Riho's, her life would be forfeit.

Seeing Riho's anxious look, Micona grinned. "You realize the position you're in, then, Riho Flavin?"

"Yeah, but I suspect we're thinking very different things."

At this point, Phyllo appeared behind them, hauling lumber in both hands.

"......Then Master wins this competition," she declared.

"What do you mean?" Micona snapped. "I've had enough of your delusions."

"...Master gathered all the lumber and rock here. He felled cedar and beech trees this morning and fetched the rock from the quarry."

Micona looked at Lloyd.

"Oh, it's not a big deal, really." He seemed sheepish. "Unlike treants, cedars and beeches don't fight back, and I just helped carry the rocks. That's the least I could do!"

Micona appeared to have frozen to the spot.

After a long silence, she managed a confident smile.

"Well, it seems you've won the warm-up match, but the real battle starts here! Just you wait! Retreat!"

With that, the entire group turned and ran away.

"Well, she hasn't changed..."

".........Mm."

Riho and Phyllo both shook their heads.

Then a cheer went up from nearby. It seemed the king had arrived for an inspection.

"Hello! How are things progressing?"

Despite the threat from Jiou, the king had stood his ground, remaining resolute—and word of this had spread through the armed forces, dramatically increasing their faith in him.

A series of proclamations had followed that prioritized the safety of his citizens.

"To avoid war, we must ally with other countries to stand against Jiou.

"We will do everything in our power to keep the burden of this from affecting your lives."

It was a far cry from his frightening demeanor while a demon lord had possessed him.

"Thank you, one and all. I know this is hard work, but I believe this is the best option to avoid the chaos and crime that too often go hand in hand with refugee scenarios. I imagine this will be but the first of many trials in the months to come, but rest assured, we are utilizing your labor for the peace of Azami!"

He still had a bit of a tendency to lean into the jargon, but this much they could overlook.

Now he was pushing someone else to the fore.

With such force that he almost tripped—Allan, looking very uncomfortable.

"Huh? Ah!"

"And even if we do find ourselves at war, we've got Allan and his compatriots on our side!"

Allan stared out at the crowd with fear in his eyes. "Um, compatriots?"

This, of course, referred to the Kunlun villagers. Their arrival at the stadium was now officially Allan's doing.

"No need for modesty! Your strength is the strength of those you lead. Be proud!"

"No, no, no, no, I don't even know those people! C-Colonel Chrome! You know I'm not that strong, so why is this still happening?!"

Chrome gave him a pat on the back, shaking his head.

"Explanations are far too hard. I swallowed that porcupine fish."

"You did?!"

"Well, I skinned it, gutted it, stewed it in miso, and chewed it thoroughly…"

"That's no different from ordinary food!"

If you remove the needles, the skin is actually edible, even tasty! But he *had* kept his word, even asking the fishmongers how to prepare it so…anything to avoid having to explain that the village from children's stories really existed.

"You're just being lazy! I-Instructor Merthophan, you tell him!"

Merthophan and Choline were standing next to Chrome. Mertho-phan had saved the king and been given his old job back.

He simply shook his head. "Allan, I am no instructor."

"Huh? Then what…?"

"I am a special teaching liaison from the Ministry of Agriculture, Forestry, and Fisheries. Hey, make sure you get that pavement even! Rice needs to breathe!"

It seemed he had not resumed his old teaching job, but instead become some sort of military intermediary. He was now supervising the grain warehouse construction with the same ferocity he had once put cadets through their drills.

"…I'll use what I've learned farming, pay the villagers back one day—and turn Azami into the world's leader in agriculture!"

Can't fault him for ambition.

Meanwhile, Choline was clutching her head.

"Why did I ever fall for this guy?"

Next to her was Rol—in an Azami military uniform.

"You had awful taste back in school, too!" She smirked.

"Shut up! Rol, I got you this job! You keep it if I say so! Remember that!"

"Scaaaary. You'd have only yourself to blame for missing out on my skills."

"For bribery?! You're a snake!"

"I said from the start I was here to do what you can't do! Nitwit."

Mena stepped in to settle them down.

"Now, now, finish this up in court; you can definitely win there."

That was less settling them down than adding fuel to the fire. Hav-ing her former boss working under her seemed to tickle her pink.

"I see the uniforms haven't changed anyone…," Riho said. When she smiled at her almost sister, there was a touch of the child she'd once been.

"Yup! Merthophan was all, 'I shall be a farming evangelist! And all the wheat and rice raising I'd foisted off on him are all *my* job again.'"

"Eep, Chief Alka?"

"'Sup, kiddos. Lloyd doing well?"

Twin tails bouncing, Alka went flouncing over to Lloyd.

Selen hissed at her like an angry cat. "What do you want?!"

"Just taking a breather!" Alka glanced out toward the surface of the ocean. Marie was floating out there, looking like she'd come to settle a grudge left over from the Kunlun visit.

"A breather? Looks more like she's not breathing!"

"What are you doing, Chief?!"

Lloyd sprang into action, pulling Marie out… In the processes he ran on water, but everyone was past caring about these trifles.

"Are you okay, Marie?"

"Oh, Lloyd! I must be in heaven…"

"You aren't! Stay with us!"

"Lloyd, in my final moments…I should tell you I'm really the princess…"

"Don't be ridiculous! You're not a princess! The princess would never live on canned food when I'm not around!"

Her very being refuted, Marie went limp.

"Oh, dear! I think she's delusional!"

He finished her with a death blow.

Lloyd made up his mind. This called for drastic measures.

"I have no choice…I'll have to give her mouth-to-mouth!"

Some phrases are basically bombs.

"""Stooooooop!!""" all three girls yelled as one.

Lloyd flinched. "Er, why?"

Selen made a beeline for him, trying to peel Marie out of his arms.

"Sir Lloyd, this is madness!"

"S-Selen? Do *you* want to give her mouth-to-mouth?"

"No! I absolutely don't!"

She stopped pulling and let go. Marie had been all stretched out, but now she snapped back to her original shape, groaning.

"…Let Riho handle it. I'll take care of yours, Master."

"Why?!"

"*I* wanna get Lloyd's mouth-to-mouth!" Alka yelled. "I'm drowning in love! Oh, that was actually pretty clever."

Micona came racing in from very far away, scowling. "Mooooooooo-ooooooooooooooouth-to-mouth!!!!!"

"Didn't you just finish running away?!"

Riho was really on her comeback game today.

The king was absently watching over all of this. "Allan," he said, "could you call those underlings and have them settle things down here?"

"I...I don't think anyone could solve this mess, not even the heroes of legend."

Nothing could stand in the way of the war for Lloyd's lips.

It was like asking someone to settle a battle between lions over a single serving of meat.

One such lion was inches from stealing Lloyd's lips.

"Just you watch, Eug! Sou! Shouma! I won't let anyone ruin my fun! I'm gonna keep this world intact and control the Last Dungeon that way!"

Alka's words were lost amid the chaos. This group cared more about Lloyd's chastity than they ever would a threat to the world itself.

Afterword

My first RPG was *Dragon Quest V.*

I didn't even know about grinding. I just plowed ahead, blowing all my spells, made the first monster I found a regular—all your classic "how not to play" type of moves.

In the middle of that game, you've got to cross the mountains to reach the kingdom…but those mountain paths are filled with things like the Wight Kings, zombies that paralyze you. Rough stuff for a kid new to video games. I remember barely staggering to the top of that mountain.

At last, I reached a village, brought my dead companions (and wife) back to life, and started exploring the town. And something a tourist there said hit me so hard, I've never forgotten it.

NPC: "Man, it gets harder to climb this mountain every year."

ME (in grade school): "You climb that every year?! Past all those Wight Kings?!"

I'd barely made it to the top alive, so his words sounded like a brutal pilgrimage. Goowain (Slime Knight) appeared equally astonished.

I believe that memory led to the creation of the village outside the Last Dungeon.

Thanks, everyone! I'm Toshio Satou, and I may have made jokes about my hair loss, but it all came back, to my great delight! Hooray for steroids.

I want to thank you for purchasing Volume 5 of *Last Dungeon Boonies*.

First, the formalities.

To my editor, Maizou—I know you're always busy, but I can't tell you how grateful I am for your help.

To my illustrator, Nao Watanuki, your illustrations are always a delight. The character designs this time were particularly rough, and for that, I'm sorry. When I got the sketch for that farmer, I knew it was the greatest design in history. I made it the background on my phone.

To the manga artist, Fusemachi—I'm grateful for your work every month. Congrats on the new print run!

To the writers who started with me, before me, and after me, thank you for all of your advice. Our conversations allow me to, however briefly, forget about my deadlines.

To everyone in editorial, design, business, and retail...and all my readers, I would never have made it this far without your help. Thank you so much.

It seems I will be able to keep this series going! I am as astonished by this show of support as anyone.

I hope we can meet again in Volume 6! I'll do my best.

HAVE YOU BEEN TURNED ON TO LIGHT NOVELS YET?

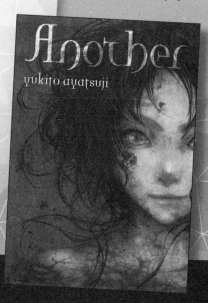